Revenge of the Bone Witch

N.I.T.R.A. SERIES

KERRY KELLER

LYNX PUBLISHING

About the Author

Kerry Keller has an addiction to caffeine, swearing, sarcasm, and has no filter when talking in public. As an avid reader to escape the drama the world throws at us, she finally got the bug to write a story she would love to read herself.

Being at the mercy of the voice in her head, she plans on writing more than just paranormal. Anything from fantasy to contemporary, to bully romance to best friends turned lovers, she plans on writing it. As long as the characters behave. She's often found yelling back at them and getting strange looks in public.

When not writing books, you can find her working in women's health care, in college, or being a single mother to a very sarcastic pre-teen boy. She swears she's a bad influence to him, so if you cross paths in the future with him... #sorrynotsorry.

Stalk Me,
It'll be a blast!

Come join the reader group to talk about the world of Purgatory Prep, get sneak peeks, and see what's to come next.

Lynx's Minxes-KK's Reading Group:
http://www.facebook.com/groups/kkslynxsminxes

Join my newsletter for teasers:
https://landing.mailerlite.com/webforms/landing/t5m6a6

TikTok:
https://www.tiktok.com/@kerrykellerauthor

GoodReads:
https://www.goodreads.com/author/show/
20923324.Kerry_Keller

Instagram:
https://www.instagram.com/authorkerrykeller/

Cover by: Everly Your Cover Designs

Formatting by: Yours Truly-KK

Developmental/Line Editing: Cassie Hurst

Proofreader: Jillian of Locke & Key Proofreading Services

This book is for the person who puts up with the obnoxious, wild, and crazy friend that can't be reined in. Thank you for putting up with us and taking off the leash so we don't choke to death!

CHAPTER 1
It's Only a Few Bruises

RAVENA

Shouts of excitement rang out in the open arena as punches were exchanged between the competitors on the mat, but my eyes were sizing up my own opponent across the room. He had a few inches on my five-foot-nine frame, and I couldn't help gazing over his toned physique. His muscles flexed as he peeled off his gray hoodie leaving a tight black wife beater that showcased the fine layer of sweat that had collected from his earlier fights.

Vic Walker. One of the top Reapers in training, second only to me. That's just a fact—one that placed us against each other for our final test.

He rolled his shoulders, leaning forward onto his knees, and caught my eye before sending me a wink. His heterochromia green and brown eyes traveled over my body in a slow perusal as I had done, but I knew where his mind was going. It was on the pile of clothes we would be leaving on the floor after this...his muscles flexing beneath my hands as I explored his body and licked the sweat off him. Hmm, how I would love to ride him like a cowgi—

"I know that look," Kaye said, sitting next to me and pulling me out of my fantasy. "Definitely not a professional one." The gorgeous redhead, and my best friend, gave me a knowing smile. I cocked an eyebrow and leaned back onto the empty row of seats, glaring at her.

"So, sue me." I clucked my tongue. "I like looking at my prizes before I pulverize them." I shrugged but couldn't stop the slow smile from appearing, sending both of us into a fit of laughter.

She mimicked my position and pulled her arm across her belly, bringing my attention to her wrapped appendage.

"What the hell, Kaye! What did Jay do to you?" I sat up and reached for her arm, only to stop inches away.

She gave me a small smile as she shrugged, then grimaced when she moved her arm too fast.

"It's not broken, so that's a plus," she answered, but I wasn't satisfied. I had watched part of their earlier match, and Jay got in a sucker punch right when the leader called time, claiming he missed the signal, but I'm not stupid nor do I think that was when he had hurt her. No one would dare speak up unless Kaye did first, and she had a bigger heart than anyone here.

Thankfully, my other best friend trotted in with a turkey leg hanging from his mouth. Thorn was my "pet" fossa that I received on my seventh birthday by accident. My parents didn't intend to walk out of the Belfast Zoo with an exotic animal for me. Who ever does? But when they found out I could hear his thoughts and communicate with him, they *kindly* insisted with the zoo staff.

I now knew they got away with it because of their money and standing with the government. Either way, I was grateful that I'd had him by my side for the past thirteen years.

'No,' Thorn huffed, 'but it's sprained, and she's not supposed to use it for at least two weeks,' he supplied through our mental link while he climbed up the bleachers and plopped down in front of us.

"So, you're out of commission for two weeks?" I gave her a pointed look.

"How in the hell did you—" She turned and glared at Thorn. "No more treats from me, you snitch."

'Suits me just fine. It's not like I don't know where your stash is. I'll just help myself.' He snorted and tore into his turkey leg.

She's lucky she couldn't hear him, and I was not up to playing interpreter. I was too busy looking for Jay in the stands.

Kaye sighed and kicked the side of my leg.

"Give it up, Rave. Jay's still in the infirmary being treated," she informed me. "What did you do to him anyway?"

"I have no idea what you're talking about." I gave her an innocent look, but she just raised a perfectly arched eyebrow.

"Oh really? Because he showed up there as I was leaving and I caught word he had a concussion and a possible broken tailbone at least." I bit my cheek to keep the small sinister smile from creeping on my face, but it was futile. "He'll be sitting on a doughnut for a while," she added, leaning into me and laying her head on my shoulder. "Thank you."

"You're welcome."

Jay was an asshole and made it his mission to prove that Kaye and I were nothing but pampered princesses because of our parents. He'd been that way since he came to the academy five years ago. So, I figured it was my job to dish out karma when we got paired together in another round of matches after he got lucky and sucker-punched Kaye.

"I should have done more," I murmured.

"Oh, stop it. You're as bad as Thorn," she teased.

3

"Well, if I had Thorns teeth, I would have done worse damage," I insisted, reaching for my water bottle.

"Did you tell her?" she asked Thorn, nudging him with her boot.

I gave him a pointed look as he growled. *'Tell me what?'*

'I couldn't find a bathroom, so I used his cot as one. With him in it.'

I spat out my water all over Thorn, and he quickly scattered to the other side of Kaye with a hiss.

'Damnit, Rave. I've already had a bath this month,' he grumbled.

"Seriously?" I asked, wiping my mouth with the back of my hand. "Man, I wish I was a fly on the wall to have seen that play out."

"Oh, don't worry," Kaye said, her eyes gleaming with mirth. "I have it on video."

"Clarke. Walker. You're up," one of our instructors called, bringing my attention back to the center of the training ring. The area was cleared of opponents, and all eyes were divided between Walker and me.

"It would be a shame if it was played during our graduation ceremony." I winked and stripped off my jacket, tossing it so it landed on Thorn.

'Hey. Watch it,' Thorn hissed.

'You love it.' I chuckled in my head as I approached my opponent.

"So, Clarke. Are we on for the normal bet? I win, and tonight I find you on your knees?" Walker teased in his sultry voice, just low enough for us to hear. His blond curls sprung up and down as he bounced on the balls of his feet, while his heterochromia eyes sparkled with mirth. The smug bastard.

The only way he would find me on my knees was if I was tying my boots. Losing to him during our sparring matches in the week wasn't such a big deal since it was for training. This was for our finals, though, and I needed all the points I could get. Although, I couldn't pass up a wager against the sinfully cocky Walker.

"Sure, but it's you who will be worshiping me on his knees," I said, pulling my high ponytail tight before taking my spot on the floor.

He smiled and cocked an eyebrow as he found his place opposite me.

"You're just lucky we didn't get guns," he said, and I rolled my eyes so hard I saw stars.

"No luck about it. They just wanted a fair fight."

Walker wasn't lying. If we were using guns, my ass would be grass, and someone would be munching on it. Walker was a natural when it came to firearms of any kind and never missed his target.

"Okay, guys. You know the drill," my favorite trainer, Mikhail, said, walking up to us. "You've been tested on all other aspects of training, and today is your final on hand-to-hand combat. Each hit is a point, but a takedown ends the round and announces the winner. So, take down your opponent any way you can, short of killing them. If you're knocked out of the ring, you are eliminated, and your opponent wins. Good luck, and may the best Reaper win." Mikhail gave me a slight smile when he passed.

Stretching my arms over my head one last time, I took a defensive stance and blew Walker a kiss. He dropped into his stance seconds before Mikhail gave the signal, and Walker pounced like a lion on a gazelle. Too bad I wasn't as defenseless as one; I was more like a damn badger with a bad attitude.

Walker was a flourish of punches and kicks that I blocked and returned as we danced around the arena. I dodged the fist thrown at my face but took the other one aimed at my ribs. My breath wheezed out of my lungs while my ribs burned from the connected punch. The arrogant smile on the blond asshole as he bounced on the balls of his feet only spurred me on more. Normally, his green and brown eyes mesmerized me in the bedroom, but here, under the floodlights in the outdoor fighting ring, it was anything but.

"I finally thought of a way for you to reward my win while you're on your knees tonight," Walker said as his eyes scanned my body, causing a chill to run down my spine.

"Oh, you think you already have the win?" I quirked an eyebrow while throwing a quick jab that he spun away from.

"Oh yeah! I'm up four points, and you would have to win by knockout." He smirked.

Shit. He did have a point. Cheeky twatwaffle.

"So, had enough, Clarke?" Walker mocked, throwing a jab that I blocked.

"Just getting started." I huffed and grabbed his arm, yanking him towards me. Before he slammed into my body, we staggered into an arm and neck hold. I swept his leg out from underneath him, and instead of breaking free, I crashed down with him. Of course, I expected him *not* to give me the upper hand. It's a good thing I liked being on top.

We both rolled away and sprung to our feet. I quickly took in my surroundings as Walker ran a hand through his short blond curls to move them out of his eyes. The outdoor training quad was packed since I was called for my final set. And knowing my luck, it was probably televised. I hadn't paid attention to my surroundings and had allowed myself to get backed up into one of the corners. *Fuck!*

Actually, if I wanted to, I could blame this on Thorn since my lazy partner was supposed to be looking out for this kind of shit. What was the point of him being my guardian slash friend if he didn't do his job!?

'I heard that!' Thorn hissed through our mental link.

'Good!' I screamed back.

Before I could berate him further, Walker was on me with

a few precise punches that I blocked. He grabbed and twisted my arm back, pulling me into his chest, and puckered his lips, making kissing noises. Unamused, I kicked his inner thighs to make him break his hold, but he didn't budge. The close proximity didn't allow me to hit him any higher, and judging by his smirk, he knew he had me.

"Tap out, and I'll pick you for my assignment," Walker offered as he held me tight.

I scoffed and raised my eyebrows instead, knowing it would throw him off. "Sorry for the headache."

"Huh?" His eyebrows squished together as his jaw went slack.

I leaned into him, bringing my right leg all the way up and over my body from behind, and slammed my heel into his cranium, perfecting the scorpion kick. There was a brief second when I saw the whites of his eyes, and his grip on me slackened moments before his pupils rolled back as he crumbled to the floor.

The whistle blew, and cheers rang out as I straightened, smoothing out my loose pants and tank top. I held my head high, feeling smug as I walked over to where I had left Kaye, Thorn, and my bag when one of the trainers called out.

"Alright, Reapers. You have an hour to clean up and meet back in the Ops room for your scores and assignments."

"If they can," Kaye commented, and a few girls chuckled as they walked by. I glanced over my shoulder in Walker's direction and smiled at the scene. One trainer waved smelling salts under his nose while another opened a medical bag.

It's only a few bruises, brush it off and call it a day... pansy.

CHAPTER 2
Steamy Showers

RAVENA

The scalding hot water flowed down my back, relieving my sore muscles, and a very un-ladylike groan left my throat. Thankfully, I didn't have to worry about my near-orgasmic noises offending or arousing anyone. I was hidden away in the alcoves, the special showers reserved for the elites and higher-ups in the agency like my parents.

No, I wasn't considered one, per se. I still needed to graduate after this last assignment to be a full-fledged Reaper, but I wasn't about to subject myself to the communal bathroom where novice and tracker showers were when I didn't have to. There were separate showers for the graduated Reapers, but I had heard they weren't much better when it came to the pranks. And before you say anything, I wasn't ashamed of my body or cared who saw me, but—

A high-pitched shriek rang out down the hall, and I shook my head before diving under the water to drown out the laughter that was sure to follow.

Where was I? Oh yeah, those showers were often the showroom where most pranks were pulled. Rosie, one of the younger Reapers in training, a tracker, still had traces of yellow dye in her hair from last week's incident. I hadn't been subject to any of the pranks, but I wasn't taking any chances by showering in there. I did my first week in training, but when Thorn overheard some of the guys talking about putting bleach in my shampoo, I made the decision to exercise my right. Since I had been accused of being a pampered princess, why not use the perk?

But no one would dare to fuck with the alcoves and risk getting demoted or, worse, kicked out of Reaper training. The elite was comprised of trainers and agency leaders, who frequently came to train or watch us, and these showers were reserved for them.

As I rinsed the conditioner out of my hair, I blindly reached for my facial cleanser when I felt a feathery light touch slowly caress up my thigh. A chill shot up my spine and along my fevered skin. I froze as a forearm snaked between my breasts and gently squeezed my throat. A hard, wet body pressed against my back, causing my pussy to clench around nothing.

"Where did you learn that move?" Walker's breathy voice fluttered over the brim of my ear as his thick cock probed against my backside.

"Now, why would I tell you all of my secrets?" I teased with a smile and spun around to face my partner in crime...? My fuck buddy? Let's just call it what it was... complicated. He grabbed both of my wrists and pinned them above me, pressing my back against the cool tiled surface.

"I thought we didn't keep secrets." His pecs flexed under the searing spray of water before it cascaded down his abdomen.

"Aww, now there's where you're wrong," I said, enjoying

the display before me and allowing him to keep his hold. I could easily break it, and he knew it, but that wasn't the kind of fun I was looking for at the moment. "A lady never tells all her secrets."

He let out a deep and hearty chuckle as he reached over and turned down my blissful shower to a medium burn.

"Since when do you consider yourself a lady?" he growled.

The light scruff along his jaw scraped against my delicate skin as his tongue paved a path for his breath to flutter up to my ear. His free hand slightly brushed my jaw as his thumb traced my full bottom lip. Enticingly, he pulled my earlobe between his lips and gently sucked, causing my back to arch and push my hardened nipples against his firm chest. He bit down, and a moan escaped me at the seductive pain.

Fuck!

His free hand cupped the back of my head, fingers digging into my wet locks as he slammed his mouth to mine. Sparks ignited as he deepened the kiss, and our tongues explored each other. My body flared to life like a Roman candle as he leaned into me and gently wedged his muscular thigh between my own. A hunger burned inside me as I ground against him, desperately wanting him to fill me.

Walker let out a guttural groan as I kissed up his throat and along his jaw. He ground his pelvis into mine, which allowed me to run my leg up the back of his calf, pulling him in closer. As he leaned his weight against me, I shifted and slid out between the wall and switched places with him, effectively pinning him against the wall with my body.

"I'm always a lady. I'm just more of a freak in the sheets with you." I smiled up at him and bit my lower lip as I grabbed ahold of his wrists, pinning them above him.

"I don't know if that's good or bad."

I cocked an eyebrow. "You've never complained before."

He broke my hold and reached around me to grab the globes of my ass, pulling me against his rigid cock.

"Down, boy, we don't have time," I purred, reaching for my facial cleanser.

"Aww, come on. It's the least you could do for putting me on my ass," he whined as he nibbled along my neck.

"Hmph. Serves you right, you cocky asshole."

"I'm your asshole," he teased as he grabbed my ass tighter.

"That you are, but you are right. I did put you on your ass; therefore, I won the bet. Get on your knees," I smirked, pulling away from him slightly, and pointed to the floor a few feet away from the wall. Walker's eyes heated, but he said nothing as he knelt before me where the shower head was currently pointed and allowed me to move so my back was against the wall. Raising one foot, he grabbed it without direction and placed it over his shoulder, and I shifted my weight to lean against the wall. "Make me scream," I demanded as one of my hands reached down and played with my breast.

I reached up with my free hand and shifted the shower nozzle away from us so I didn't drown out Walker but allowed a nice misting over me.

Walker wasted no time as his mouth sought out my wet cunt. My breath caught in my throat as a rush of pleasure racked my body. I tightened all over as he pulled my hooded clit between his mouth and sucked hard. Arched against the wall, my fingers dug into his wet curls, keeping him where I needed him the most.

"Fuck," I moaned. "Just like that." I ground against his greedy mouth with my mound, needing more friction than he could simply supply on his own.

His tongue worked its magic, licking, sucking, and nibbling along my slit until I was in a frenzy. Panting and almost delirious with need, Walker finally added his fingers and inserted one into my wet heat before swiftly adding another, causing my legs to buckle slightly. But being the gentleman he was, he caught and supported me by adding my other leg over his shoulder. Completely exposed and left to his mercy, I leaned against the wall as he stood up, allowing my back to slide up against the wall.

Thankfully the walls are high, or else I would be giving everyone a damn show if they popped in this way.

All thoughts were wiped away when he curled his fingers inside and flicked his tongue against my clit. I was quickly approaching my release as he licked, sucked, and worshiped me like I deserved. My legs strangled Walker's head as I bit into my forearm to stifle my groan as my orgasm raced through me.

As I came back down, Walker's arm slipped, and he almost lost his balance and dropped me.

"Don't even think about letting me fall," I hissed, not wanting to leave my blissful state.

"I wouldn't dare," he chuckled as he carefully sat me back down on the floor in front of him. He smirked down at me as he boxed me in and pushed my hair back out of my face, showing me his mouth glistening with my juices, and I couldn't help but verbally wipe that cocky look off his face.

"What are you smiling for?" I said, raising an eyebrow. "I remember telling you to make me scream."

A mischievous glint crossed his face as his eyes traveled down my body once more before he pounced on me. His hand wrapped around my throat, tilting it up, and he slammed his mouth down on mine. Greedily, he swiped his tongue into my mouth, giving me a taste of myself. Before I could give in and deepen the kiss, Walker tore himself away and spun me around so I was facing the wall. His palm gently but forcefully pushes down on my upper back, causing me to catch myself against the wall.

"You asked for it," was his only warning before he lined himself up against me and slammed into me. Thank God I was on birth control and took care of my protection because he sure as fuck wasn't using any in here.

Groans echoed as he seated himself fully in me, and I had to admit he felt amazing. It was the first time we had ever gone without protection, and I'd make sure it would be our last, but I was going to enjoy it while we were here. I wiggled my ass slightly as a reminder to get on with it.

Smack!

A sharp burning flared over my right butt cheek, and I glared at the offender. "Really?" A cruel smile was my only answer as Walker grabbed my hips and began pumping in and out of me.

Yeah, I get the point. Shut up and enjoy being ridden.

As he pumped, I drove my hips back, meeting each thrust with my own while playing with my breast and bracing myself against the wall. The only sounds in the small shower were our harsh breathing, flesh slapping together, and the water droplets raining down on us and sliding over our skin. Walker leaned over me and nibbled along my neck and back as he talked about how good my pussy felt wrapped around his cock.

"You squeeze me so good, Rave." He moaned. "Like you were made only for me," he said before lightly biting my neck and slapping the same ass cheek again, causing me to flinch from the pain.

I tried to push the *'only for him'* out of my mind because I was so close to my release, and I didn't need to think of the whole relationship talk again that I was against. This was supposed to be fun, nothing serious.

"You're supposed to be making me scream, Walker. Or did you forget?" I asked teasingly.

"Oh, I haven't forgotten." I could imagine the cocky look on his face but couldn't look as he reached between my legs and pinched my clit. Pleasure raced through my body, and my legs started to shake. His strokes became faster as he swiveled his hips, hitting the perfect spot within me. "Come for me, Rave," Walker whispered into my ear before he bit down on the soft, fleshy lobe. He reached up with his other hand to cross my body and pinch my free nipple, and I exploded. I cried out his name as my pussy spasmed around his cock.

"Fuck!" Walker groaned as he stilled behind me, his cock pulsing as he found his release.

As I leaned against the wall with my eyes closed, catching my breath, Walker kissed up along my spine before sliding out and away from me. Water flowed down my back as he turned the nozzle back to me, and I felt his hand on my lower back before I felt him slightly pushing between my legs.

"Here, let me help clean you," he insisted.

"Why, Walker, this is definitely going above and beyond," I teased, turning around and taking the cloth from him. He took a stumbling step back, and his eyes widened slightly before his brows furrowed, but I gave him a wink and cleaned myself.

He tried to hide the hurt on his face, but I had already seen it. Before you call me heartless, he already knew what this was between us. I had never led him on. As a Reaper, we're solo operatives until we make higher ranks and take field office assignments. Then we could have a chance to have a family. There's no way I was ready to settle down in a relationship. All I was willing to have was a fling or the fuck buddy relationship we had, or at least I thought we did. I might have needed to reevaluate this if he was unwilling to keep to our agreement.

"You're gonna be late. You wouldn't want them to dock points now that you're below me," I razzed. He hip-checked me effectively, pushing me out of the way.

Well, I guess I'll just wash my face at the sink.

"You might have won that, but I still beat you on the

weapons course," he mocked as he started to lather soap over his chest and lower abs.

My eyes followed his movements, and it wasn't until he cleared his throat that I realized I had stopped what I was doing and was staring.

"Want another round?" He gave me a wink, and I snorted in reply.

"Don't flatter yourself. It's just been a while since I've gotten any good dick," I said, reaching for my towel.

"Whatever," he scoffed. "What do you call what we just did?" he said, aghast.

"Yeah, and I said *good* dick," I teased, blowing him a kiss before stepping out of the alcove.

I chuckled to myself as I heard him curse my name. I couldn't make things easy on him. Where would the fun be in that?

CHAPTER 3
The Living Legend

RAVENA

I walked into the Operations room and found it packed. There were only a few of us who needed to be in here since we needed our final assignment before graduating, but it wasn't unheard of for the lower ranks to assemble here. It was just another way to learn about the creatures that run unchecked in our world. I found Kaye off to the side at the back of the room, eyeing a group of younger class novices in their black and gold training uniforms gawking around the leaderboard. Every week, we went through assessments to get new placements. By the time we graduated, depending on our rank and points, we would get a buttload of perks. Most Reapers would be fighting for higher pay, longer vacations, or picking which office they would live in. Me? I was just looking forward to picking my team, which would consist of Thorn, Kaye, and me.

I made my way over to Kaye and took in her stance. She

seemed relaxed as she leaned against the wall, but there were slight lines around her eyes.

"You okay?" I asked, mimicking her stance.

"Oh. Hey. What's up, Rave?" She gave me a small smile, but it didn't reach her eyes.

"Okay." I sighed and stood up straight. "Who's ass do I need to kick? I just left you less than an hour ago, and someone already decided to pick a fight with you?"

"Heel, Fido," she joked, and my body relaxed slightly.

"Don't you ever say that in front of Thorn," I hissed, winking to lessen the threat.

"Deal. *If* you don't go on a warpath."

I perked up. "So I do need to kick someone's ass."

She grabbed my arm and pulled me back to the wall. "No. Dad just pulled me off to the side and wanted to reassure me that not taking an assignment today wasn't going to affect my final placement," she admitted with a frown.

"I'm guessing that wasn't very assuring." I knew her as well as I knew myself. We both hated handouts, and having her father give her one on a silver platter was more of a slap in the face than the offering he intended it to be.

"Yeah." She turned to face me directly. "Since I got hurt and Dad is... well, Dad, I passed, but you won't find my name up there." A frown and a crease appeared between her eyes as they darted to the board. "The only way I'll get an assignment is if someone will pick me even with my bum arm." She scoffed. "Might as well put me out in the pasture."

"Oh, please. You're dangerous with both of your arms out of commission. Anyone would be stupid to pass you up," I said, squeezing her shoulder reassuringly. "You know we're a team until the very end. No matter what state we find ourselves in."

'Who are they betting on today?' Thorn asked, breaking my

moment with Kaye. He leaned against my five-foot-nine-inch frame as I gave him an annoyed look. I knew he was an animal and all, but I knew for a fact his memory wasn't *that* bad. The novices were doing the same thing they always did in this room.

'*I'm pretty sure it's the usual,*' I countered.

"Hey, Clarke. You in?" Walker called from the front of the room. I hadn't seen him up there, but I watched as he ran his fingers through his short blond curls, sending water droplets flying, wincing as he hit the area I knocked him out at.

How did he beat me here?

He shook it off before his heterochromia eyes shined with mischief once again, raising his eyebrows at me in question.

"You know betting is against the rules," I said, smirking at him and a few others who turned my way.

"That is right, Clarke," our training leader Cassie said as she strolled into the room with the confidence of a woman who knew her worth. Her brunette hair was pulled back into a sleek bun, and she looked sharp in her all-black leader uniform as she went straight to the front, causing a ripple effect as all of us came to attention, even Thorn.

It was comical seeing a predator close to six feet long with his tail making up the majority of his length, a cat-like head, a short dog-like muzzle, and large rounded ears, sitting at attention. But what was weirder was the fact he was my friend rather than a pet. Having him here wasn't a big deal since some Reaper families were known to imprint on animals. Those types of animals were there to serve and protect their Reapers. So, most Reapers just thought I was the first in my long Reaper family line to inherit the gene that allowed me to imprint Thorn. That's all they needed to know about our bond, because if they knew the truth—that we could communicate telepathically—questions could come up because that wasn't normal for an imprint bond. There were a select few people who knew of the unique ability I had with Thorn.

Basically, Kaye and her parents were the only ones outside my family.

Cassie was our Operations Leader and top trainer at Nightmare Interference Tactical Reaping Agency, or N.I.T.R.A. for short. She had a reputation for being a hard ass when it came to training and didn't believe in cutting corners. Her next statement led me to believe she *allowed* certain things to slip past her, but she was always aware of them.

"But I'm sure you do it anyway," Cassie said, turning and clasping her hands before her. Her hazel green eyes scanned the room before nodding, allowing us to relax.

"Okay, Reapers, today we have five assignments, and there are only twelve of you that are eligible. So, either team up or pray you scored high enough that you can pick an assignment on your own," she said as she turned to her high-tech computer system and started typing.

Thorn led the way as we slipped through the five groups of trainees to the front of the pack to take in the leaderboard. I'd only slipped to second place once, but that was because I had a bad day and fought with my emotions instead of my head. I haven't made that mistake since.

"I know I'm on top, so who's pairing with me?" Walker called out, and I rolled my eyes so hard I blacked out for a moment.

Finn, Walker's friend, spoke up. "I'm in. I know I bombed my last training test, so I need the points," he confessed.

"You on top? Pftt. No way. You would have to beat Clarke!" Mikhail exclaimed, walking into the room behind us. As he walked past, I stuck out my boot, and he bumped it in solidarity before joining Cassie. Mikhail was one of my favorite trainers, and I guess you could say a friend or more like a big brother since I could remember. He ran his hand through his short red hair before sending me a wink.

"Besides, you know I'm always on top, Walker," I said,

then dropped my voice to whisper, "Twenty down that I beat your ass once again."

"Deal!" he agreed, right as the ranking board flashed and the new ratings appeared. Clarke, Walker, West, Le'Vey, and Lopez.

"Fuck. I didn't even make the top five," Finn whined.

'*When has he ever?*' Thorn huffed and rolled his eyes at the brunet.

'*Good point.*'

"There are your rankings, and here are your last assignments before graduation. At number five, we have an unsanctioned vampire in Memphis that's been posing as the late Elvis Presley. Don't ask because I don't know," Cassie said as a few hands shot up in the group. "He needs to be contained and delivered to the Eastern facility."

There were N.I.T.R.A. facilities worldwide where doors would send the Supes back to their original dimension, Purgatory. In this case, the Eastern facility was the closest place that could handle this Supe.

The next two assignments were tame compared to the ones I'd done in the past. A Brownie in Fort Lauderdale, which was a pixie that loves to clean, was pissed that they asked her *not to clean* a hotel room while an investigation was in progress and was rioting in the laundry room. Rumors were starting that the place was haunted, so they needed her taken care of, else they were going to lose business. Also, a bear shifter in Nashville was badly injured in a show of dominance, and they were having problems healing, so they needed to be transported to the nearest facility and sent back to Purgatory. *We aren't always the boogie men.* A demon had crossed over and was currently loose inside a mental hospital, which piqued my interest until Cassie mentioned the last one.

"And for our number one spot, we have the local legend back from the dead—Julia Brown. And she's pissed. She's threatening to erase the rest of the 'bigoted' South with the storm that's brewing in the gulf," Cassie said.

"Are we supposed to know who that is?" Finn asked.

"Well, I see who wasn't paying attention in my class last week." Mikhail shook his head as Finn blushed for being called out.

"That's the Bone Witch that wiped out a small town north of New Orleans back in the early 1900s... when she died," Walker explained. "Are you saying she's alive in Ruddock?"

The thought of the old Bone Witch hiding out for the past hundred years kinda excited me. *Now, this is the case for me, and since I'm ranked number one, I get first dibs.*

"I thought her death was faked, and she was cast out of Earth, never to be allowed back because she killed all those people years ago," West asked as he leaned against a wall.

"Either way, I doubt she's here legally. I mean, why else would we be here," Walker said arrogantly.

"A good point, Walker," Cassie stated. "Priestess Tanda actually gave us this tip when a few of her customers told her about the disappearances in the swamp and people going missing. Apparently, the numbers are astronomical."

"I'll take her case," I said confidently.

"Are you sure?" Cassie asked, cocking an eyebrow. "This isn't a cozy assignment. You'll be traipsing through the swamp in inhospitable weather."

"Yep."

"Okay then. Are you taking anyone with you?" she asked.

I sent her a smirk and looked down at Thorn before smiling at Kaye.

"You know my team only consists of Thorn and Kaye," I said with a brief smile.

"You might want to reconsider. She's not one to play

around with, and Kaye is supposed to be on bed rest," Cassie said with a worried tone in her voice.

"I can still work with one arm. I'm not a complete invalid," Kaye spoke out with a growl.

"We got this," I stated confidently. *She will see. My team always completed the job.*

CHAPTER 4
The Crescent City

RAVENA

I grimaced, pulling up to the rundown building with a lone rusted brown pickup truck out front. My McLaren stuck out like a sore thumb, but I wasn't going to pass up a chance to drive my second baby. Since my parents had a few houses around the States, they insisted on having a car there for me. And when it came to assignments, they came in handy. God, I hoped we didn't have to stay here long. We didn't think to get an updated tetanus shot before we left. And by the look of this place, this was probably where that whole myth of getting herpes from a toilet seat came from. The breeze slightly rocked the lone shutter that drooped from the hinge of the front window. Dark clouds could be seen to the south, and they looked like they were rolling in with the storm that was brewing. Glancing back at our destination, I could imagine the building once stood out like a bright yellow beacon, but the faded strips of color hung as if it had given up on life and was waiting patiently for its turn to move on. By the looks of it, Julia might not need her full strength to completely wipe this spot off the map. I didn't know how it was standing on its own.

'*Are you sure this is it?*' Thorn asked as he poked his head between the front seats of the car.

"Are you sure you didn't accidentally type in Bates Motel into the GPS?" Kaye questioned as she took in our surroundings.

I glanced down at my GPS and back up at the building that looked more like an old hut than a motel. "This is the right place, guys. But we're not staying, okay? We're just looking for someone from Frenier."

'*But according to the GPS, that's miles away from here,*' Thorn pointed out.

"Yep, I know it's miles from here, Thorn," I answered out loud for Kaye's benefit. "But that place was destroyed in the 1915 hurricane, or did you sleep through that lesson?" I gave him a knowing look, and he snorted. "The locals mentioned that this is where I could find the last relative of the only survivor of that hurricane. But you were probably too busy stuffing your face with beignets," I said, unbuckling my seat belt and opening the door.

The humidity instantly hit me in the chest, and I leaned against the side of the car for a moment. It might have looked like I was waiting to let Thorn out, but in reality, I was trying to get used to breathing in the air's moisture. I was from the Midwest, not the Deep South. This was a different type of heat. Hell, even the locals said it was hot for this type of year.

"Fuck this heat," I murmured and quickly put my hair up into a messy bun. No matter how straight I got it, with this humidity, I was sure to be sporting an afro puff within the hour.

'I agree. I already feel like a cheap whore,' Thorn said as he hopped out of the car and looked around.

'Those are probably the only ones that come here,' I said, gritting my teeth at the bare establishment.

"Holy shit. This afternoon heat is going to fry me to death. Here, can you help me with my hair and spray this on my neck?" Kaye asked as she came around and turned her back to me. I quickly pulled her long red hair up into a messy bun so it was off her back, and sprayed the bug spray on her neck. She was a bullseye for insects. She kept the bugs off me, but she would swell up like a balloon if too many got to her.

As she grabbed her backpack from the trunk, I took a closer look around. The whole place was surrounded by old Cypress trees and gravel. The old *Vacancy* signpost only spelled *can*, which I took as a positive omen.

I used the end of my trusty leather jacket to wrap around the rusted door handle and opened it long enough for Thorn, Kaye, and me to slip into the building. Dark hardwood paneling and old green shag carpet met us as we walked in. Then, there was the stench of mold and old cigarette smoke, which practically made me gag as we walked up to the unmanned counter.

'There's a wet spot here that smells like blood,' Thorn pointed out as he sniffed a darker part of the floor and gagged.

'Well, it's a good thing I'm not here to investigate that,' I said and looked up when I heard shuffling. An older gentleman in overalls walked out of the back room. His skin looked as though he'd never used sunscreen a day in his life. Old and leathery, to the point I couldn't tell if he'd had too much sun or was naturally that dark, just a few shades darker than my sepia skin tone. I doubted he was wearing anything below those overalls either by the glimpse I got of him scratching his balls.

He eyed me up and down, then gave Kaye a short glance before spitting out his chew.

I hoped there was a spit bucket down there, but from the *splat* and Thorn's reaction, there wasn't.

"We don't take no pets," he said as a greeting. His voice was rough with a deep southern twang I'd heard in the South before. I pulled my jacket around me as a chill ran down my spine that wasn't coming from the AC. By looking at this place, they wouldn't have known what an air conditioner was. "They gator meat."

Okay then.

"I'm not here for a room. I'm looking for Jules Cormier?"

"Wa look'n fer Jules?" a voice trailed out from the back room.

"I'm handlin', Pa," the man in front of me yelled back without taking his eyes off me.

'Thorn, how many people do you smell in this place?'

'Rave, all I can smell is shit. Like literal shit, so I'm no help. And what the fuck did he say anyways? Is he speaking English?'

'Creole. There are about 10,000 people that speak Louisiana Creole, and I just found two of them,' I sighed.

Before I could say or do anything else, a whirling of a machine preceded a man in an electric wheelchair. A dark and worn handwoven quilt took up most of the wheelchair, leaving red slippers peeking out of the bottom, while a mop of wispy gray hair was combed over to hide his baldness. Sun spots and wrinkles littered his sun-kissed hand that was exposed to drive the wheelchair. He had a scarf that matched the quilt wrapped around his throat that only allowed his bulbous nose and hazy white eyes to peek out of his covering.

'Shit. He's blind.'

"Ain't no blind, kid. Cataracts."

'Can he read our thoughts?' I asked Thorn as I tried to keep from blushing.

'Pfft. No, dipshit. You said that out loud,' Thorn teased.

Kaye shuffled, and I caught her giving me a disapproving look.

Well shit! Give me a break; I thought my filter was in place.

"Uh...sorry. You just caught me off guard. I'm looking for—"

"We 'ear ye. Dat be me. Want ya want?' The old man turned his chair to face me, his scarf dropping low enough to show the scowl on his face.

His intense, milky eyes gave me goosebumps, and I froze for a moment. Thankfully, Kaye didn't have that problem.

"Hello, sir. We were hoping to get the exact location of Julia Brown's old shack," she spit out like a pro.

"Don't wanna go there. Nothing but gators 'n ghosts," the younger man said, leaning on the counter and giving her a leer.

What's his problem with her?

As he leaned forward though, he did answer the question about what was under his overalls. He was as naked as the day he was born. Or, given the state of this place, he was grown in a petri dish. I felt like I needed to scrub off all of my skin just from standing in this place.

"Oh, we know. It's the ghost we're looking for. A couple of the locals said our best bet was to come here and ask for Jules Cormier and not the local bayou tours," I said, raising my jaw in defiance and pulling the attention off of Kaye. These guys weren't going to scare us off with ghost stories; that was our job, and ghost stories were what excited us. It's what we lived for.

"Local tours won't take ya near there, no ways. Just take yers money," the man in the overalls spit out along with another wad of dip.

Eww.

Well, I'd obviously found Jules, but he didn't look like he

was in any shape to help me get to Julia Brown's supposedly haunted shack out in the bayou.

'What are you thinking, Thorn?' I asked my bestie.

'Maybe just ask him what he knows about her?' Thorn advised me.

Hmm. He did have a point. I leaned on the counter and made a mental note to dry clean this jacket immediately when the sleeve hit something sticky. I couldn't get out of here fast enough.

'Being this close to the ground is unacceptable, Rave. Pick up a few gallons of bleach and stain remover when we leave here. I need a scrub-down stat!'

'Believe me, the view up here isn't much better.'

"So, does this mean you'll take me out there?" I batted my eyes at the younger man.

"Don't do tours," he replied, and I felt Jules' eyes boring into me.

"Hmph. Figured as much. Come on, Kaye. They probably don't know anything about Brown anyways," I mumbled, but I knew they could hear. Before I could take a step, Jules spoke up.

"Now, waits a minute."

"Pa—"

"Don't pa me. Ole' Brown needs da go. She's tun'n up these here swamps fer too long. Besides, she done near wiped out the LaComb family," he snapped at his son before turning his milky eyes back to me. "Well, come see," he said, nodding at the break in the counter before heading back to the room he came out of.

His son let out a long sigh before he ran a hand over his thinning hair. "Sure hope y'all know what yer doing, else y'all be more gator bait," he warned before lifting up the counter-top, exposing a passageway.

He didn't wait for us before turning and following his

father out the back. I gave Thorn and Kaye a doubtful look before taking a leap of faith and seeing where this rabbit hole led.

'*We're going to die,*' Thorn predicted, and I had a feeling he might be right.

CHAPTER 5
She's a Klunker

RAVENA

We shuffled through what I could only guess was a building full of relics of times passed. There were mountains of junk everywhere. Now, I knew I had no room to talk if you saw the backseat of my car right now, but in my defense, I spent *a lot* of time in it, and at least you could see parts of the floor. If it weren't for the entrance to this place, I would have no idea what the floor or walls looked like in here.

Along the floor were busted-up boxes that Mr. Jules weaved his electric chair down. One of the towering stacks of papers almost toppled over, and my life flashed before me. Thorn was notoriously known as a busybody and liked to put his nose into everything, so it spoke volumes when he stuck to my boots like glue.

'*I don't trust this place not to reach out and suck me into its moldy depths to be lost forever,*' he said when I asked him why he was clinging to me like a toddler without a binky.

I tried to suppress the cough that sat at the base of my

throat as I inhaled the layers of gunk in the room. *My lungs will never be the same after this place.* A newspaper clipping from the New Orleans *Times-Picayune* caught my attention when I saw 'Aunt' Julia Brown named. I glanced up at the date, and my eyebrows disappeared.

'*What is it?*' Thorn asked, feeling uneasy that I had stopped our progression.

"Hey, Kaye." I reached out and grabbed her arm before she could continue on. "There's a newspaper here from 1915. How old is Jules?" I asked, wondering, not for the first time, who this man was.

"He must be pretty ancient to have that," she replied, looking down at the stained yellow newspaper.

We quickly caught up as they exited the building and stepped onto a patio into the scorching heat. The chaos of junk continued along the deck, out across the lawn, and into the weeds.

Thorn pushed against my legs and almost tripped me as I tried to step away.

'*What the hell, Thorn? What's wrong now?*'

'*We're not alone out here. Something is hiding out in those weeds. Pick me up... please,*' he begged.

'*I'm not going to pick you up.*'

'*Either pick me up, or I'm gonna climb you.*'

I peered down at my bestie and was taken back at him, shaking with fear. He met my eyes and shook off his fear by lifting a paw, flexing his claws, and showing his intent. I rolled my eyes as I picked up my massive scaredy cat.

'*Fuck. You need to lay off the sweets,*' I murmured as I shifted his weight so I could continue walking.

'*You need to lift more weights. You're getting fluffy in the middle,*' he retorted as his tail poked me in the gut, making his point.

Yes, I was squishy in the middle, but I liked my curves and

carbs. Plus, Walker didn't complain when I had him beneath me. Thorn curled his weight around my shoulder to see as we reached a section where the path opened to a dock where two boats were stationed and Kaye was waiting.

"Last time I checked, he had working legs," Kaye commented when we caught up.

"Yeah, I thought so too, but someone's being a scaredy cat," I informed her.

I moved so I could look at the boats that gently rocked against the pier. I recognized them from the many advertisements for swamp tours around here. I had been on one once when we took a trip to the Everglades when I was little, but all I remembered was that it was loud and fast. You know the ones I'm talking about. The boats with flat bottoms and big propellers inside the metal cages that speed you across the water. The other boat looked more or less like an old raft or canoe.

Jules stopped at the edge of the dock and pointed to the raft. His son quickly went to work to pull the decrepit floating wood pile up on the overgrown lawn. A grunt escaped me as Thorn shifted, and his claws dug into my waist. Thankfully, I was wearing my jacket, or I would have been sporting a new scar.

'*Thorn, I can't do this anymore. Look, we're out in the open. If something were to come for you, you could escape before it came close.*'

'*You're a lousy friend,*' he whined.

'*And you're the weakest link. Goodbye,*' I said as I dropped him and rolled my eyes as he landed on his feet.

As I joined Kaye, Jules asked her to hand him a wooden box on the pier's edge. He opened it, and inside was a worn and folded piece of paper.

"E'res a map," he said, handing out the paper.

Kaye gently opened it and showed me the crude drawing.

How the hell are we going to find our way with this? There was a bunch of water and land masses, but besides that, I had no idea what the hell I was looking at, and I said as much.

"The swamp is the only way to get there," Jules's son retorted.

"It's okay, Rave. I think I can figure it out and follow it," Kaye said as she looked at the bayou before us and back at the map.

'*Sweet, so we can use the Gater Bater then,*' Thorn cheered as he hopped like a ferret to the big motorized boat with that name sprawled across the back.

"Don't know where yer going, little feller, but if yer going after ol' Julia, you can't go in that. She'd hear ya a mile out," Jules said, nodding his head toward his son. "Junior's just makin' sure the pirogue's in top shape 'fore ye head out," Jules said.

Thorn immediately stopped hopping around and turned, giving Jules an evil eye. '*But if we go into that other monstrosity, we'll sink!*' Thorn pouted yet moved away.

"Smart little critter," he said in surprise.

'*Well, I guess we'll go down as a team, bitch. Now come on.*'

I hated to admit it as I mustered up my own insecurities, but Thorn was right; we were probably going to sink.

"She's alright," Junior called, standing back up and approaching us. "Lantern has fresh batteries, and oars are freshly slick," he addressed his dad before turning to us. "Just need your deposit before ya go."

"Deposit?" Kaye asks, eyeing the floating wood pile.

"Have to replace the equipment when you don't come back."

Well damn.

"How much?" Kaye asked.

"Grand," Junior said.

"A grand? For that floating hunk of junk?" I sputtered out.

"It's an heirloom. Been in the family since the beginning," Jules murmured.

'Since the beginning of time, maybe. Rave, it's a dinosaur's toothpick. It's not worth dirt,' Thorn whined.

He had a point, but at least it wasn't *my* money I was shelling out. It was the agencies. I reached into my jacket and grabbed my wallet as Junior's greedy eyes watched my movements.

"I plan on getting at least half of that back when we return," I grumbled as I handed over the cash into Junior's meaty palm and walked over to Kaye. She was cautiously studying our mode of transportation.

"We might die before we get there," she whispered.

"Thorn has the same thoughts," I replied, keeping my voice down and our proprietors in my sight.

"And you don't?" Kaye questioned as she used her boot to gently push on the boat.

Junior walked over and held the boat secure as Kaye, Thorn, and I cautiously entered and got situated. Jules' eerie eyes tracked our movements, and if I didn't know better, I would say there was something 'otherly' about him.

"Anything in your car we should worry about if you don't return?" Junior smirked.

"Don't get any funny ideas about my car. It's a transformer, and he'll eat you if I don't come back," I hissed, making Junior flinch.

Kaye let out a nervous chuckle and gave him a reassuring smile.

"Don't mind her. That car is her baby. But we do have someone coming to pick it up if something happens to us."

"Good luck. Hopefully, you just run into Julia's shack and miss the LaCombs. Either way, there's a storm com'n in. It'll be dangerous on the bayou," Junior said as he pushed the boat away from the dock.

I grabbed the oar and tried to figure out how to paddle properly. This wasn't something we went over in class.

How to survive the bayou 101. Nope, never was a subject on our ever-changing syllabus.

Shit, we might die out here, and it wasn't going to be from wildlife or the witch. It was going to be because neither one of us knew how to operate this damn thing.

CHAPTER 6
Pitted Wetlands

KAYE

W e were off to a shaky start, and I didn't just mean the way we were rocking the boat.

"Calm down, Thorn, you're not helping," Rave hissed as the boat slightly rocked. Thorn's legs sprawled out in a panic as he tried to stabilize himself again. The wind was picking up, and with Thorn constantly trying to balance as he stood, he was going to cause us to tip over, which was not what any of us wanted.

When Junior saw us struggling, he took pity on us and took a few minutes to show us how to use the pole and oars. He also went into more detail about the LaCombs. If the rumor was true, they had fallen under Miss Julia's spell and did her bidding. So not only did we have to worry about her, but possible civilian casualties and/or hostages. But that was for later.

Rave decided it was best for her to handle the pole and oars since my arm was still healing, and I wasn't going to fight her. I knew once her mind was made up, it was almost impossible to make her change it. Although, with how she was grunting and fighting with the pole, I'd bet she wished to take back her words.

"Come here, Thorn." I beckoned him over and gently petted him until he settled. "Just lay down and try to relax. You moving around is shaking the boat." Thorn laid down but kept raising his head to look over the edge of the vessel with dilated eyes and sporadic breathing. I threw Rave a look in question, and she snorted.

"He doesn't like not seeing his surroundings."

That made sense, I guess.

"Okay, how about this, Thorn? You pay attention to the trees and sky around us, and I'll keep my eyes on the water and shore that you can't see."

He snorted and just stared at me. I swear he even arched an eyebrow.

"See, I have to do it anyways since I'm navigating," I said as I waved the map before him. He let out a small growl but averted his eyes toward the trees.

"Why the trees?" Rave asked.

She probably thought I was just placating Thorn, but we were in the middle of swamps where anything could happen. My biggest fear was snakes dropping onto us, and I told her that.

She snorted again and rolled her eyes.

"Don't laugh. I've seen videos where snakes have launched themselves from roofs and trees and landed and just slithered away. You, out of all people, should know that not everything is black and white."

"Are you serious? They launch themselves?"

"Yep, like a trapezist at the circus." I pursed my lips and watched silently as Rave glanced up at the trees and shuddered.

There was something about the Southern wetlands that was magical. The low-hanging moss and the gentle lapping of the water were almost relaxing.

Slam.

What the hell?

"What happened?" I asked, looking around the area but not seeing anything out of place besides our new location.

Instead of being out in the middle of the river, we were suddenly underneath and up against a cypress tree. I reached out to try and calm Thorn as he bolted up and shook the boat, glancing around. I really wasn't looking forward to swimming in the bayou.

"I— I don't know," Rave answered before checking to her left. "Ugh." She groaned before raising her boot and kicking at something on the other side.

"Woah, you're rocking the boat," I yelled.

"Thank you, Captain Obvious! I didn't realize that's the action I was doing." She punctuated each word with a kick, getting angrier as she went. Her brunette hair was starting to come out of her messy bun. Mumbling a few curses under her breath, the boat shifted and started to float away from the tree.

"Oh! We were stuck on Cypress knees," I said as I finally got a view of what was sticking out of the water.

"Whose knee?" Rave asked, and I sent her a disapproving look.

"Cypress. They grow up from the tree's roots and stick out of the water. Some say they help stabilize the trees against a hurricane and maybe aid in respiration for the trees that are constantly in water," I said proudly, finally able to put my knowledge to the test.

"How the fuck do you know that?" Rave screeched.

"Well, I studied up while you got your nookie on between the library and the abbey again," I chuckled.

"Shit, you could see us?" She sent me a shocked look

before pushing off with the pole once again. "I could have sworn we were far enough away from the light that no one could see us, " she mumbled.

"You were, but your screams probably woke up the whole academy."

"Damn it. I knew I should have gagged Walker with his shirt. He wouldn't know how to stay quiet even if our lives depended on it."

Smiling to myself, I turned my attention back to the map and noticed we were almost to another turn-off when we started drifting back into the trees.

"Damn it!" Rave grunted and viciously smacked the water with the pole out of frustration.

"Having problems, Rave?"

She threw the pole back into the boat and ripped off her jacket while I held out my hand to catch it as that, too, was thrown to the bottom of this floating wood pile. Her bracelet was also on the floor, which also spoke volumes of how upset she was that she was throwing her precious jacket around and didn't notice her bracelet came off, especially out here in this dump. I slipped the intricate metal into my bag for safekeeping while her face pinched in anger.

"Fuck this damn swamp!" she shouted. "I don't know what the hell is going on, but all of a sudden, I can't control where we're going," she said as she wiped the back of her hand across her forehead and roughly redid her messy bun.

"What do you mean you can't control where we're going?" I laid her jacket down beside me and stared up at my bestie.

Rave glared back, and if looks could kill, I would be ashes right now.

"Just what I sa—"

The boat suddenly swayed so hard that I dropped the map and reached for the edge to hold on. My foot pushed Thorn back down to keep him from flopping around, and that's when I heard a splash.

I looked around but didn't notice anything out of place. A growl ripped from Thorn's body, and he shook me enough to dislodge my foot so he could lean over the edge of the boat.

"What's wrong with him, Rave?" I asked while trying to pull him back to me. "Rave?" My head snapped up, looking for her, and it was then I finally realized she was missing.

Shit.

Rave surfaced a few feet away, sputtering water. She blindly reached around for the boat as her hair was plastered to her face and covered her eyes. "Motherfucker... piece of— what the hell hit us?" Rave cursed, forcibly pushing her hair out of her eyes before taking my hand and getting into the boat.

"Is that why you fell over?" I asked, taking in the swamp water and some green stuff clinging to her.

"No," she growled, picking the green slime off her shoulder. "I decided to jump in and finally try one of those mud baths I've heard so much about." She pulled her tank away from her body and wrung it out with a sneer. "Thankfully, I took a dip without my jacket," she mumbled to herself.

"Okay, I don't need the snarky quips. I'm sorry that your mud bath didn't work out like you wanted, but obviously, something is going on," I said, grabbing the bag between my feet and throwing her a towel. Don't ask why I had one; it was just a hygiene thing.

Before turning my attention elsewhere, I felt a thump at the bottom of my feet.

"Did you feel that?" I asked, freezing in place.

"Yeah," Rave answered, wiping the water from her face. She pulled moss from the side of her cheek before looking down at Thorn and immediately glared at the opposite side of the skiff.

"What?" If I had fur, my own hackles would be raised as I popped the holster of my Smith and Wesson handgun sitting in my bag. Thankfully, I was ambidextrous and could use my weapon with my left. I wasn't as good as Walker when it came to firearms, but I could hold my own.

"Thorn said we're not alone." She leaned over and slowly dropped the towel, keeping her eyes glued on the same spot as Thorn. She fished around for something in her coat pockets, making enough noise to wake the dead.

"What are you looking for?" I hissed, keeping my words low.

"Honor," she whined, then growled in frustration, which made her sound more like a stuffed pig than anything resembling words. But I knew what she was talking about. Honor was the name of the bracelet she received as a gift when she was just a baby. According to her parents, she almost died in an accident, but a guardian angel stepped in and, with his intervention, saved her. Of course, it wasn't a normal bracelet. Not much was known about Demfire, only that it wasn't found on Earth and it was powerful. In Rave's case, since it was infused into her bracelet, it allowed her to change it into a weapon of her choice. Luckily, her Demfire-infused bracelet was still in my bag from when I had caught her jacket earlier.

"Chill, I have your Honor," I mocked.

A shadow passed over my bag just as I reached for it, making me pause and lean back in time before a huge snake landed on us, separating me from the rest.

The snake was so massive that not all of his body could fit on the boat. From the coloring of the blotchy yellowish scales, my guess was it was a ball python. But how was it that big? And what was it doing here? It lunged at Rave, but she dodged its attack barely.

Wait, that wasn't right. Ball pythons weren't naturally aggressive. Without another thought, I reached for my gun between my legs, stood up, and fired off two shots into its back. Its head whipped around and hissed, which was out of character for the snake. Before I could take aim again, something tightened around my ankles, making me lose my balance. I slipped back to my seat, dropping my gun in the process, and found the snake's tail wrapped around my ankles.

Shit. This was more than an average snake. Instead of freaking out like my instincts were screaming at me to do, I took a quick breath and froze. Yep, I'm the badass that freezes when snakes drop on them. Another hiss had me looking back up, and I found Thorn swiping a clawed paw at the snake and Rave swinging the pole around to battle the snake like the avenging angel that she was. I saw my gun peeking out from under the snake's massive coils around my feet, so I shifted them enough to reach for it.

I fired off a bullet into the bindings around my ankles, and thankfully, they released enough that I stood up and moved toward the action at the front of the boat. Hopefully, I wasn't going to tip us in the process. Obviously, this snake could take pain and bullets, but I wanted to see if it could handle my adjustments to my toys.

I was a Reaper through and through, but my real passion was weapons and ways to improve them. Ever since I saw Rave's gift, I was fascinated with the idea of improving and combining weapons where I could.

I pushed the button on the side of my gun and drove the butt of it onto the top of the snake's skull just as it reached back to strike. The knife that I had manufactured to extend sunk into the skull with an audible crack. With a quick twist and a plop, I pulled out my weapon in time to see the black eyes turn milky white before it hung over the boat's edge.

"Well, I think it's dead now," Rave said, kicking the lifeless body as it started to slip into the water.

The body started to get lighter and change before our eyes, revealing a very naked dead man.

"Holy shit!" I gasped.

"Wow. Yeah, you would think with how big he was, he would be hung like an anaconda when in reality it was a garter snake," Rave said as she watched his legs slip over and into the murky water.

"Oh my God! Is that all you think about?" I whisper shouted at my best friend.

"Obviously not!" She snorted. "I'm also thinking how lucky my ass is that I'm not in the water right now," she said and pointed to the opposite bank, where two alligators slipped into the water.

Swallowing back my retort, I nodded and grabbed my towel to clean my weapon. I took it back; this place wasn't relaxing at all. It was a fucking nightmare.

CHAPTER 7

More Than a Master

THORN

R ave quickly pushed us away from the feeding frenzy that ensued where the snake shifter had died, turning down the left bend that Kaye instructed.

'I bet he was a snake because he was a yellow-bellied coward.' I chuckled to myself. *'Did you see the size of him? I bet the only thing he could get busy with was a thimble.'*

For all of my effort, Rave just rolled her eyes and kept a straight face. *How dare she? She knows what I'm giving her is golden.* I whipped my tail back and forth aggressively, but I didn't care if she noticed that I was getting upset. It was a good way to release my anger instead of spiking out like a pufferfish on steroids from Hell. I still couldn't believe I looked like one of those when I got angry. *Just another thing that set me apart from a normal Fossa.* I had always compared myself to a porcupine, but apparently, my fur didn't stick out that far, and I couldn't launch them at the enemy.

Ha. Wouldn't that be funny, me running after the enemy,

sending three-inch quills hurdling at the screaming lunatic as they waved their hands in the air, wafting their ungodly B.O. about?

Speaking of B.O— *'Um, Rave... you know you stink, right?'*

A growl ripped down the connection before she slowly turned her focus onto me. I blinked rapidly and stuck out my tongue in the way I'd seen those domesticated dogs do, hoping to ease the sting.

'You know, we're in the bayou...you really don't need *your fur, do you?'* She smiled cruelly.

'You know, if I peed on you, it might neutralize the smell,' I offered.

'How about I just throw you over, and then you won't worry about smelling me. We can be twinsies.'

I curled my lip, growled, and walked over to Kaye, lying down by her feet. At least she didn't stink, plus she would pet me when I wanted it.

Kaye started running her long, deft fingers through my fur for a few seconds before going back to her weapon. I swear that thing was already clean two minutes ago. Between Rave steering us to the Wicked Witch of the Bayou and Kaye polishing the metal off her weapon, I was getting no love around here.

"Why do you think he attacked us?" Kaye finally spoke, pausing her polishing and stroking that puuurfect spot behind my ear.

'He was probably a spy for the witch. A look out for her and to slow us up. He smelled familiar. I think he was at the house, in the weeds,' I supplied while I was in bliss.

Rave relayed my words, and my blissful mood jerked to a halt.

"Really?" Kaye asked and gave me a quizzical look.

'Yes! Now get back to petting me. I need a rubdown. This stress does NOT do well for my fur.'

Rave snorted.

"Do I want to know what he said?"

"No."

'*No.*'

She shrugged and focused back on me, which I definitely wouldn't complain about. "Hmph, either way, you're probably right, Thorn. Good thinking," she said. Her deft fingers worked wonders on my shoulders, and I couldn't help but settle down, close my eyes, and relax as they talked.

Their continued banter was a gentle reminder of how lucky I was to have them. The family that rescued me from a certain death. Without the Fates stepping in, I would probably be decaying somewhere six feet under. Wait. Or would they have just fed me to a lion in another enclosure?

That day, thirteen years ago, still lives on in my vivid memory.

I was trying to play with my brothers and sisters, but they would purposely leave me out. I thought it was because I was the runt, but now, looking back, it was probably the fact I was different.

There weren't many people out staring at us, so it was easy to hear when they did come by.

"The sign says Fossa*. They are carnivores from an island in Africa. Madagascar," a man told the woman and little girl that was with him. I could only guess he was the father.*

"Oh look, sweetie. There are babies," the older woman squealed in excitement. Yep, she had to be the mother. The little girl was holding something that floated in the air as she peered in, but I didn't pay too much attention to them. I went back to dealing with my own issues.

'Oh, come on, guys, I want to play too. Stop leaving me out!' *I grunted. One of my brothers pounced on me and bit down hard on my ear, making me cry out, before taking off and leaving me by the watering hole.* 'Now you're just being mean.

It's not fair.' *I whimpered and turned my back on them as they continued to play.* 'Fine.' *I sniffed,* 'I'll just play in the water.'

"They are adorable. Don't you think?" the older woman dressed in a flashy suit observed.

"They're assholes," the little brunette girl replied, grabbing my attention. She was looking at my siblings as they pounced on each other.

"What?" the father questioned, raising his voice and grabbing the young girl by her shoulders.

"Ravena Abigail Clarke!" the mother scolded the young girl, but she didn't apologize.

"What? It's true," the girl said with spunk as she looked between me and my siblings. "That's why he's pouting and sitting by the water. They're being mean to him."

I glanced up and found the young girl pointing right at me. Shocked that she had caught that, I quickly backed up and lay down in the tall grass. I learned from the past that there wasn't really a way to communicate with the humans that came to see us, so why try? If anything, if they thought you could understand, they poked and prodded you to death to make you do tricks for god-awful food or praise.

No, thank you. I'd had that done to me for two weeks until I learned to stop responding how they wanted me to. There was no way I was going to call attention to myself once again. No, sir, no way. I'd learned my lesson. I grimaced as my stomach growled and cramped, causing me to curl up in a ball and lay my head down on my paws. Hopefully, our trainer that came in here would actually have something to feed us that didn't make me sick.

Soon enough, Mother called us into the inner dome to eat. I walked in and immediately groaned. The stench of raw beef and mice made my stomach roll with unease. Again!?! Where was the variety around here? They were going to starve me to death. There was an undertone of something else that smelled good though, but I couldn't pinpoint what it was. Why couldn't I have that?

As my siblings devoured the food before them, I remained off in the corner, watching the debacle in silence until I heard the young girl's voice coming down the hall. It wasn't uncommon to have a few vets or handlers come in and see us. But we never had young humans come in to observe us this close.

"Does everyone get to come back here?" the young voice carried into the room.

"No, honey. We're special because your father donated and built this section of the zoo. Your grandparents own this," the mother explained as they walked in and gave me my first up close look at our visitors.

The young girl was wearing pigtails and was dressed in a silver jumper and boots. The item she had been carrying was no longer with her, but she didn't seem upset as she scanned the room. "Wow!"

"Come see, Ravena." Her father motioned her over to where our handler was dishing out our food in the form of rolled-up balls of meat and placing them on tree limbs to have us climb up and get them.

Boots clomped on the concrete floor before tiny hands, and her brunette mop of hair appeared over the fence, taking in the sight. A bright smile bloomed across her face as she watched my siblings playing tug of war over a mouse while my mother tore through some meat.

"Hello, Mr. and Mrs. Clarke. I'm Rachel, and this must be Ravena." Our handler turned to smile at the visitors and bent down to the little girl's eye level. "Happy birthday! Did you want to see the Fossas up close?"

She nodded and showcased a missing front tooth.

"Very well. They are almost done eating, and as soon as they are, I'll put the mother in a separate area. Safety first!"

"What's wrong with that one over there?" the father asked, pointing directly at me, causing two sets of eyes to swing my way.

"Mommy, can I see?"

The dad hoisted the little girl up so she could lean against his hip as she peered at me. I sniffed the air and found a pleasant lavender and vanilla scent. Nothing like the smoke-filled scent of the handler that was in the room.

"We've tried different birds, meats, and nuts, but he either won't eat it or keep it down. Sadly, it's not sustainable to keep him on a feeding tube for the duration of his life," she said mournfully.

Maybe if you wouldn't bring me raw garbage, I would actually be able to keep it down.

I don't know how she initially did it, but as her parents bent their heads together, the girl's voice reached out to me.

'Aren't you hungry?'

'I'm starving, but the food they give me is gross,' *I admitted as I cocked my head to the side.* 'How are you talking to me anyways?'

'I don't know,' she replied with a shrug. 'But what would you like to eat? Maybe I can get it for you.'

Her mother leaned down and lowered her voice, "Sweetie, are you talking to him now?" Her eyes swung between us.

"Yes."

My stomach rolled at her admission, reminding me that I was once again going without food. Poop. I'm in trouble. What if she tells the handler and they bring the needles again?

"Ah," the handler said, standing up and walking over to a section in the wall. "If you want to expedite the process, there are footies by the door that go over your shoes. Once I return from putting momma in the other room, I'll get us started on properly washing our hands before touching the babies. I'll be right back," she said, coaxing my mother away and disappearing into the other room.

'If you were serious about helping, I don't know what it's called, but that lady was eating something that smelled good,' *I confessed.*

"Daddy, can you put me down?" she asked, squirming until she was free. She ran over to a counter and grabbed a container of what looked like grass. That couldn't be it. *"He's hungry and wants what's in here," she told her father, holding up the container to him.*

"Ravena, are you sure?" A deep line appeared between her mother's eyes as she took her daughter in.

"Yep, trust me. Besides, it's my birthday."

"You know that can't work all day long, right?" Her father sighed and shook his head with a small smile playing on his lips.

"But it will work now, right?" she asks, smiling and lightly shaking the container in her hands. "Please! He's hungry."

Her father looked resigned as he looked over her head in the direction of where my mother went before he quickly picked up and placed the girl on the other side of the enclosure with me. Once her feet hit the ground, she let out a little squeak of excitement as she ran over and squatted down in front of me, not coming into the grass.

'Is this what smells good?' *she asked, opening the container before me.*

I eyed her cautiously from my hiding spot, but a strong cramp from my stomach prompted me to follow my gut. I carefully emerged from my spot and climbed onto her lap before sniffing the container.

'Mmm. Yes. Gimme!' *I lunged for the container, but she moved it out of my way and bopped me on the nose.* Are you kidding me? I'm a downright killer here with...baby teeth and freaking claws of fury, and she's whacking me on the nose? How dare she!

'Say please,' *she urged as she brought the container closer and grabbed something big and white from the pile of grass.*

'PLEASE!' *I bounced on the edge of the container, my caution of the tiny human forgotten. She gently pushed me back as she tried to keep the container of grass from spilling.*

'Does this smell good?'

I sniffed and nodded, gently taking the object out of her hand. It's the least I could do since she did bring me something that smelled delicious. 'Mmm hmm.' *My cheeks puffed out as I chewed as fast as I could on her lap.*

"Mommy? What do they like to eat?" *she asked, trying to keep her voice down. Her eyes searched through the container for more white pieces and fed them to me as she waited for an answer.*

"I think mainly meat, sweetie. Oh honey, grab that one," *her mother squeaked, and I glanced up in time to see her father swoop in to grab one of my siblings, running our way. Probably to ruin a special moment for me.*

The girl tensed up and gripped me to her as if she was protecting me from my siblings, and my little heart melted right then.

"It's okay, sweetie. We'll keep them occupied. Go on and feed him," *her mother laughed as she grabbed another one.*

The grip loosened, and she ran her hand down my neck, soothing me. 'It's okay. We won't let anyone hurt you anymore,' *she said, and for some strange reason, I completely believed her. For the first time, I felt like I was safe and wanted. There was hope.* 'How about some chicken?' *She smiled.*

'It smells weird,' *I admitted, wrinkling my nose.*

"WHAT ARE YOU DOING?" *my handler screamed, making me jump. Her face was red with fury as she hurried back into the room.* "You can't feed him that. You'll make him sick!"

The little girl's dad jumped up, my siblings forgotten, and stepped in front of the handler as she angrily pushed her stray hair out of her face. My new friend pulled me close and grabbed another round white piece out of the box, feeding me the morsel.

As I swallowed the item she gave me, my curiosity got the better of me. 'What's going on? Why is she mad?'

'I don't think I was supposed to feed you,' *she answered honestly, giving me a pout as she looked down at me. My heart skipped a beat as it dawned on me that I might lose my new best friend as soon as I met her.*

'But why? My stomach finally doesn't hurt. Isn't that a good thing?'

Her mother came over to us and gathered us in her arms. I was trying not to panic as her father tried to calm down the lady I'd known my entire life.

"I don't care who you are. You can't just disobey rules. I'm calling security and management," *my handler threatened and reached for the phone. She pressed a button and started to bark out harsh words.*

"Suits me just fine. I need to make arrangements for this animal anyway," *he told her, pulling out his own small phone.*

"Mommy? What's going on?" *the little girl asked, shaking as she held me tight.*

"Don't worry, sweetie," *her mother whispered. "I think we just found you the perfect present. It looks like you're getting a new friend as a pet. How does that sound?"*

The smiles on both of their faces were enough to make me understand that my life was about to change forever. Since then, Rave and I had been inseparable and pretty much fought like siblings.

It wasn't until Rave spoke up about the time that I realized I had dozed off.

'*Fuck*'

Rave accidentally let that word fly through our connection, and I cracked an eye to peer over at her.

"Kaye, how much longer do you think we have before we get there?" Rave asked, worry laced in her voice.

'*Wanna share with the class?*'

'*No, not really,*' she growled.

I chuckled to myself, knowing she was going to spill anyway.

"My guess is the sun would still be up a little bit longer if it weren't for those clouds rapidly closing in. It will be dark soon." She let out a heavy sigh. "I was hoping we would have been heading back before the storm came in or it got dark," she admitted.

"Yeah, that would have been nice, but instead, we're going in blind, in more ways than one," Kaye agreed. "I might as well get the lamps out and lit so we don't get caught out in the dark."

CHAPTER 8

A Spoonful of Sugar Helps the Alligator Go Down

RAVENA

We turned the last bend, and my stomach sank as the moonlight shone down upon the horror in front of us.

"Is that what I think it is?" Kaye asked as she set down her lamp. I slowed our boat down to a stop to stare at the monstrosity before us.

'Yep. It's our death. I knew we should have taken the psyched-out Demon in the mental hospital,' Thorn whined.

I couldn't blame him since we were facing a massive alligator skull before us, the likes of which should only have existed in a cartoon. The jaws were open and towered above some of the branches of the bald cypress trees.

"Is there any chance that's petrified wood in the shape of a massive jaw?" I asked no one in particular.

'Sure, and I'm the fucking Easter Bunny that farts sunshine and glitter.'

I rolled my eyes and snorted.

"Well, according to the map, that's the way to go, but that landmark isn't on here. So, I'm placing my bet on the fact Julia put that up recently."

"That would be my guess, or else someone would have to be pretty damn blind to miss a massive skull sticking out of the woods if they were looking at this from an aerial view." I quirked an eyebrow in her direction. "So, we're possibly looking at a ward?" I asked, knowing I was probably right. Some supes tended to look down on wanting to go back to Purgatory. They tried everything in their power to stay here on Earth, even warding their territory to warn off intruders or, more specifically, Reapers.

"Yep. We might as well arm up. Who knows what we'll face once we hit her ward," Kaye said as she started digging into her bag.

"Let's put on your first line of defense." I smiled and held up a bottle of bug spray. "Reapply?"

"Good thinking!"

After we sprayed ourselves, I threw Thorn's back and neck armor on him. Safety first! Kaye had found a material strong enough to protect his weak points while molding and bending when he used his spikes. I swear, I didn't know what I would do without my brainiac bestie.

"Here, don't forget your meds." Kaye handed me a silver bracelet with interlocking capsules.

"Yep, can't go without this." I gave her a smile as I snapped the small metal piece around my left wrist since Honor took up most of my right wrist and forearm. If there was a ward, it would cause us extreme nausea to the point where we would be forced to turn away. With those bad boys, that would be a thing of the past with the medicine-infused metal. Just to be on the safe side, I fasten one on Thorn's back leg. He'd never needed one before, but I didn't want to take any chances.

I strapped a few throwing knives into my thigh guards,

and inside my jacket were a set of dampening cuffs. Purgatory supplied them to us to help suppress magic users.

"Remember, Rave—our goal is to find, suppress, and transport, one, Julia Brown, to the nearest door back to Purgatory for her trial."

"Yes, moooom," I mocked.

"Oh, please. You know if I didn't remind you every time, you would go in there, guns a blaz'n." She chuckled as she picked up an extra bullet clip and attached it to her belt. It didn't look anything like her normal clip.

"You're such a party pooper. What's with the clip?" I nodded my head at her belt.

"Tranqs. New weapon with some of that dampening spell that's in the cuffs. I'm trying them out." She smiled proudly, her bright white teeth shined in the moonlight.

"Sweet. This should be an easy case," I said under my breath as I picked up the pole and pushed us closer to the massive skeleton.

'Suuuure. If you don't count the fact we've already been attacked by a snake shifter, you've taken a dip in the swamp, it's dark as a black hole, the winds are going to either carry us away or swallow us up, and the witch we're after is out for revenge on the people she thinks *wronged her. Sounds like we should have asked for a raise.'*

'We? Don't you mean I *should have asked for a raise?* You *don't even get paid.'* I internally groaned as soon as the words left my mind.

'Yeah. About that. Why aren't you paying me?' Thorn demanded.

'Hmm, let's see. I already pamper the shit out of you. I feed you—well, get you takeout—give you a home, listen to you mock and berate me, put up with your shedding, and give you a comfy ass bed to sleep in, yet you always take MINE. But the main

reason is you can't use a debit card,' I rattled back, and I could practically hear him roll his eyes in the silence.

'Hmph. You might have a point... for now.'

I felt a slight punch in the stomach as we crossed over the threshold of the ward, causing me to swallow down the bile that ricocheted up my throat.

"Either these got weaker, or she's the strongest one we've been up against." Kaye pointed out, indicating our identical bracelets. She took a few gulps from a bottle before passing it over, and I drained the last of the water.

'There's the dock!' Thorn called out.

'I don't see it. So let me guess. It's in the one place I wish it wasn't.'

'Yep, it's in the mouth of that creepy thing.'

"Am I imagining things, or are the eyes lighting up on that skull?" Kaye's voice shook slightly.

The woman took on an overgrown snake but got scared of orbs in a skull? Sometimes, she surprised even me.

I angled the boat for the front of the jaw and glanced up, catching an unearthly green haze where the once black pits of its eyes were.

"Nope, you ain't crazy. I think she knows we're here," I said as we slowed to a stop at a large tooth. The dock was on the other side and wedged between two sharp teeth that looked to have enough room for us to slide through. I swallowed the lump in my throat as I made sure the rope we had was tied properly to the boat. *I don't want to lose this sucker and be stuck out here.*

'What kind of witch is she again?' Thorn asked, looking up at the gaping jaw.

'Bone Witch.'

'So that means she can control bones? Like the ones towering over us?' He hesitated in his movements as he waited for my answer.

"No, Thorn. You're thinking of a Necromancer. A Bone Witch just gets her power from bones, like for casting spells by wearing them. Most humans believe them to be diviners, giving them advice and never being capable of lying. Maybe Julia once was one of them, but a true Bone Witch is one that will pull the essence out of the *fresh* bones and use that as payment for the magic she needs to cast spells. In class, they talked about how every magic user has to pay a price and give of themselves when taking from the earth. Or something along those lines. She just happens to use bones for the exchange."

Kaye gave me a smile and winked as she threw on her backpack.

"It's okay, Thorn. I'll go first." She leaned onto the two sharp incisors and tentatively stepped onto the dock. Once nothing happened with the teeth, she turned her head and smiled. "See. Nothing." She finished putting her weight on the wooden planks and screamed as they sank with her body weight before buoying up to hold her. She laughed nervously, "Well, nothing to be scared of except some water."

"Here, tie us off," I said, keeping my smart-ass comment to myself for once and throwing her the rope. While she secured us, I helped Thorn cross and handed the lanterns over once Kaye was ready. It took a little longer as the waters became rougher, and I struggled to keep my balance as the boat rocked.

With my jacket back in place and Honor wrapped securely around my right wrist, I was ready. Albeit stinky with swamp water, but nonetheless prepared to take on Julia Brown. We followed the waterlogged planks further into the beast's narrow throat and nearly gagged at the stench.

"What's that smell?" Kaye cried as she quickly pulled her collar around her nose. I mimicked her and slowed my steps to take in my surroundings.

I swallowed down the extra saliva that flooded my mouth and quickly turned my head after spotting the culprit. *Okay, just breathe through the mouth, Rave... you can do this.*

"I think I know what the smell is, but I doubt you want to know," I choked out between my gagging sounds. *Don't throw up. Don't throw up.*

"Ugh. I can guess." Kaye stopped and shined her lantern in my face. I'm sure my sepia skin now had a green tint to it. "You only make that sound when you see maggots." Kay swung her lantern away from my face and, unfortunately, down onto the decomposed dog and human torso.

There were a lot of things I could handle. It wasn't the fact that their bodies looked like exploded Hot Pockets or some of their bones were missing, but there was one thing that made my stomach squirm. And she just shined a spotlight on them. I gagged and coughed, trying to will away the urge to vomit.

"Oh shit! Sorry, Rave." She quickly swung her lantern in the opposite direction, grabbed my hand, and led me toward the small opening at the back of the alligator's skull.

'Now who's the weakest link?' Thorn chuckled as he passed me.

I'm going to skin the little fucker. Or maybe push him in the water. Yep, that sounds better.

'And just remember, if you push me in the water. I'll be in the car... in your back seats... all wet... and stinky.'

An unintentional growl slipped from between my clenched jaw, and Thorn laughed, knowing he'd guessed right.

Once we passed the skull, we found a narrow, overgrown path that led deeper into the swamp.

'Well, there's no turning back now.' Thorn pressed against me, so I reached down and scratched his ear.

'Nope. So are you ready, Toto?'

'Sure, Wicked Witch.' He snickered and pulled away.

'Why am I the witch?'

'*Because Kaye gives me belly rubs when I want them.*'

'*She spoils you.*' I pursed my lips, and he stuck out his tongue. '*She wouldn't if she heard half the shit you said,*' I reminded him as we started down the path.

'*And that's why I'm taking advantage of it while I can.*' He laughed and moved up next to Kaye as she took point.

CHAPTER 9

Bones of the Lost

Ravena

The natural noises of the area were hard at work to sway us into a false sense of peace. The frogs and crickets filled the night air with their song, as well as the twinkling lights from the fireflies. Their illumination helped guide us as we crawled over downed trees and under the low-hanging brush, but it only made my anxiety rise. Overcast was blocking out most of the moon, and the heat was finally easing, but that was because the breeze was bringing the cooler air from the impending storm our way. *It wasn't going to be long before we found ourselves in a downpour.*

"Are we any closer to finding this bitch?" I couldn't help the whine in my tone.

I hated the idea that our visibility was cut down to practically nothing. And that we were in an unfamiliar area. And maybe the fact we kept on finding swampy areas where water seeped into my boots and soaked my socks. *This outfit is ruined. I'm billing the academy for this shit.*

"Here. Can you hold this light for me?"

I held up both lanterns as she fully unwrapped the map and brought it closer to her face.

"It looks like Jules marked the old town, and this small X is her old shack. So according to this, her shack should be up ahead if we continue to follow this path." She smiled up at me as she awkwardly folded the map with her good arm and tucked it into her jacket, retaking her lamp.

'Hey, guys. We got a problem,' Thorn called out and coughed for Kaye's benefit, his head swiveling around, not focusing on one area in particular.

'What's that?'

'Well, what do you hear?' He cocked his head, staring at me.

"Shit," Kaye whispered. "When did the crickets stop singing?"

Rustling in the leaves pulled my attention to the left of us. Kaye touched my shoulder and motioned for us to lower the lanterns and set them on the ground. She pulled her gun free, and I signed, "Don't shoot me."

She rolled her eyes and signed back, "You'd heal," ending that conversation.

When we were younger, we often had to be with our parents when they traveled, and we had to be on our best behavior when meeting dignitaries and their families. Since we were kids and still wanted to play and 'talk' to one another, we decided to learn a new language. The problem we ran into was our parents were hyperpolyglot or multi-lingual. So, we found the one language they didn't know that allowed us to play and stay out of trouble: American Sign Language. So, it worked for us as kids and in situations where we needed to be stealthy, like now.

'Thorn, do you smell anything?' I asked as I signaled for Kaye to move up the path slowly.

'All I smell is mold, piss, and death. A beautiful cocktail for this atmosphere, wouldn't you say?'

'Didn't need the sarcasm. Stay with Kaye. I'm going to see what's in the bushes.'

I signed the plan to Kaye, and she gave me a thumbs up. I didn't say we always stuck with the appropriate signs, but it worked for us.

I watched as Kaye and Thorn disappeared from the light and further up the path before I slowly moved back down and into the thick brush. I kept low and slowed my steps as I pulled my knives from my thighs and let my eyes adjust to the dimness. Something was stalking us, and I was going to find it.

As I slowly moved to the area we once stood, something darted out in front of me. I jumped back, stumbling over a tree root, and reached out to steady myself on the trunk when something pulled at my ankles, and my world spun.

The ground swayed before me as I tried to push my hair out of my eyes, as some of it was stuck to my sweaty face. I was upside down in some kind of trap, swinging like a piece of dead meat. This wasn't something I was expecting, but at least I still had my knives. Thank you, Cassie, for the training to hold onto our weapons when we become airborne. It was a hard lesson to learn, but apparently, it had paid off.

As I slowly rotated around, I took in my situation as the moonlight filtered through the trees. The ground below me looked clear, if not soggy, so if I cut myself down, I wasn't going to damage myself further than a few bumps and bruises, hopefully, but there was no sign of what darted out from the bushes.

I pulled myself up and started to cut through the rope holding me up when I heard it—chittering. I froze and held my breath. *No, I must be hearing things.*

Letting out my breath slowly, I made sure to try not to make any noise and swiveled my head around to look below in the direction of the noise. I could barely make out a grayish figure approaching through the tree limbs, but when it turned its head sideways, I swallowed back the bile and weighed my options. I really didn't have any, so I started cutting as fast as I could through the rope, not giving a damn about the noise. I needed to get free, or else I was dead!

I knew what this monster was, and there was no reasoning with it when it was in this form. My heart pounded so hard against my chest that I could feel it hitting my ribs, bruising me from the inside out. The chittering got louder as I sawed away at my bindings. *What the fuck is this made out of? Kevlar?* My palms were getting sweaty, so I quickly placed my knife between my thighs, holding it still as I wiped it against my pants. I couldn't afford to have my knife slip out of my clutches.

Goosebumps pebbled my skin when I looked over and easily made out their gray, wrinkled skin with open sores. The Abuhuku. A six-foot half beast, half mosquito shifter. Wild gray and white fur covered its back and legs, helping it blend into its surroundings. But what scared me shitless was its nose. It was wide and came down to a point like a razor-sharp dagger, which they used to cut through their prey's skulls and suck out their blood. They always left a dry husk of skin behind, typically hanging from a tree.

Shit. I never thought they would be here. They're not supposed to leave Purgatory, there's never been a report of them even being on Earth before, not even an unsanctioned one.

If that shifter got its hands on me, my life would be over. There were rumors that their skin was sticky and you couldn't get away if they touched you. There weren't any confirmed cases, and I didn't want to be the first. As he moved closer, I took a chance, knowing I was setting myself up for death, and flipped my other dagger around in my hand. I aimed for the Abuhuku as he leaped toward me and sent my dagger flying. It stumbled but took another step toward me, and my eyes widened in fear. I switched my knife into my dominant hand when he stumbled again, dropping to its knees and reaching for his throat. Dark liquid started dribbling out through his fingers as the sounds of gurgling reached me.

I got him! How bad I got him, no clue, but I wasn't waiting for him to recover. A cold, wet drop hit me square between the eyes. *Fuck, it's raining!* I quickly returned to cutting through the rope the best I could with the rain and dropped to the ground, which put me a few feet away from the shifter. My knife nicked him, but it wasn't a death kill. Though my thigh knives were coated with a type of powder that burned the skin, so I knew he was suffering. I found myself slightly torn—if he would just change back, I would be obligated to try and save, protect, and send him back to Purgatory. In this berserked state, my hands were tied.

Damnit, Rave... just do your job!

With my mind focused, I reached over and slit his throat, watching him bleed out within seconds.

'*Thorn, we have Abuhukus out here, so watch out,*' I warned, wiping my knives off on the surrounding moss and standing up.

The silence was deafening as I waited for a response. There was no way he could have been out of range yet. When we were younger, we once tried to see how far our connection could go when we visited my grandparent's estate in England. It was merely a few feet when I needed to go to the restroom. The older we got, our range extended. The last time we visited, Thorn and I had been to each end of their estate, about a football field in length. At that range, we could hear every other word or so. It was as if we were picking up static.

'*Thorn! Answer me, you fur bag. I'm not playing around,*' I said desperately. I needed to know they were okay.

A chill ran down my spine as thoughts of my friends in

danger whirled in my mind, spurring me into action. I fought through the foliage as my mind dredged up thoughts of what happened to them. *Did an Abuhuku get them? Are they dead? Please tell me Thorn is just pulling a horrible prank.*

I burst through the thick brush and back onto the small, overgrown path. Our lanterns were burning low with an eerie green glow where we had left them. *Well, that's not good.*

Something had obviously been at play here and changed the bright white glow of the atmosphere we had with the lamps. I left them behind since they would only attract more Abuhuku and continued down the path, scanning the area for signs of either Thorn or Kaye.

No more than twenty feet up the path, I found evidence of a struggle with muddied bootprints and broken shrubbery. Knowing stealth was on my side, I quickly but quietly followed the path of destruction. It was the blood smeared on leaves and strands of red hair in a bush with thorns that had my heart skipping a beat.

I swear to God, if my best friend is dead, I'm drying out this whole fucking swamp and watching it burn like a desert.

I climbed over a tree trunk and landed on my face, mud and all. When I pushed myself up, I silently screamed as I came face to face with an Abuhuku staring at me with milky white eyes. Slowly, I let out a shaky breath as I noticed the bullet hole between its eyes.

Well, at least I know Kaye was here. Where here is, is definitely a different story.

I was lying in a pile of blood-stained bones. As I stood up and took in my surroundings, I noticed there were no dried husks in the limbs above, so this wasn't where the Abuhuku was eating his victims. So what lured the Abuhuku and Kaye here?

Shit. What did I get us into?

CHAPTER 10
They be Zombies

KAYE

I'd known Ravena my whole life. We were sisters; blood didn't play a part. We'd shared everything—cribs, nannies, clothes, secrets, and not once did we envy each other. Even when Ravena came home with Thorn, I didn't feel left out. She was so excited to tell me about our new pet that we begged for a sleepover and stayed up all night getting to know him.

Since I'd known Thorn almost as long as Ravena, I would say that I had gotten to know him pretty well. Minus the whole telepathic thing they do. Too bad I didn't have that connection because that would have come in handy and possibly would have kept us from our predicament.

Thorn cocked his head, baring his teeth while growling at me, and all I could do was roll my eyes at his frustration.

"Will you just fucking calm down," I whispered through gritted teeth. "So, I missed your warning. Didn't you see I was a little busy killing an Abuhuku?" I huffed out and went back to studying our surroundings. I knew we were up shit creek without a paddle. When we got ambushed by a couple of men, my gun, darts, and bag were taken. Thorn's armor was left alone, at least. I was lucky enough to have kept my clothes and bracelet on; otherwise, I would have been in pain along with this frustration of being caught.

We were in a makeshift cage with wooden slabs and rope. A decent fire was burning across the lawn about forty yards away, which highlighted a small decrepit shack and the swamp. Small bones were strung up over the single window that I hoped were from animals instead of children, but I wouldn't put it past the crazy witch.

The smell of rot and old blood was unbearable, and breathing through my mouth only made me want to gag instead of calming my stomach. From where we were, I could see shadows moving but couldn't determine what was making them.

Thorn yipped and bit the side of my pants, leading me to the edge of the cage.

"I knew it wasn't just a dumb animal," a gruff yet familiar voice whispered behind my ear, making me jump.

"Fuck, where did you come from?" I turned and grabbed hold of the board between us, grateful that Junior was here. At least now he could free us.

"Now, where's the other one?" He spoke a little louder as he walked around the makeshift cage and squinted at Thorn and me. "I would have figured the mixed girl would have been with you two in the bone pit."

Bone pit? Hmm. I think the better question was, why was Junior here? He was out in the open and wasn't whispering anymore, which I suddenly realized didn't bode well for us.

"A big 'ol snake shifter came out of nowhere on the bayou. Was that your doing?" I said, completely deflecting his question but hopefully allowing him to take it as an answer. I figured I might as well try to figure out where this fucker had his hands in all this.

"Damn, guess that's where Leonard went," he said, rubbing his chin. *So, he knew the guy? Does that mean he sent the guy after us?* I eased away from the edge of the cage.

"So, was the LaComb family just a ruse?" I asked, bringing his attention back to me.

"Oh no, that was all true. That's my wife's family."

"You're married?" Why I found that a shock, I had no clue. But it apparently wasn't the smartest thing to slip from my mouth.

"Of course I am," he spit, sneering at me.

"Sorry," I held up my hands, trying to placate the man. "I just didn't expect to see you here when you were so adamant about getting rid of Julia Brown," I said honestly.

"Pfft. That's Dad. He's senile and don't see the good that Julia can do for the world. She can wipe all the bigot people from the South and start anew."

"She's a bone witch. That means she needs BONES to gather her strength to do that. Where do you think she's going to get them?" I countered.

I already looked up the missing persons report on our way down here. Depending on how many people were in this LaComb family and Junior here, all she needed to do was to wipe them out, and she was home free with enough power to do her bidding. I needed this lug to get that through his head or let me out to stop this.

"From the people I've been sending down this way. Did you really think that map was the only one? I've been making copies for years."

My stomach fell. Junior was truly in on this, and there was no way of swaying his mind.

"Hey honey, any problem getting the Reaper?" a sweet

honeysuckle voice called out behind Junior, and he smiled, turning away from me.

The feminine voice let out a squeal of joy as Junior lifted and twirled the petite girl in his arms. The moonlight illuminated her pale skin, showing the contrast of Junior's dark skin and clothes. Her strawberry blonde hair was long and flowed around her shoulders as her body glided through the air.

When Junior sat down the girl, she turned and scowled our way.

"I don't know what's so special about Reapers anyways. According to Julia, you're the boogie men of the world. You don't look all that powerful."

"And there, for a minute, you actually looked smart. But looks can be deceiving."

"Why you... little cu—" She lunged at the cage, but Junior grabbed her by her waist, stilling her movements.

"You know she will turn on you, right? In her past, she's never worked with others. She uses people and then disposes of them," I tried to explain to them, but I knew by the look in their eyes they were a lost cause.

"Junior, Lily. Come on. We ain't done yet," someone called, pulling their attention away from us. I watched as a figure walked toward the small fire that burned in the background. They set down a cauldron and beckoned the bayou dwellers from Timbuktu.

"Coming, Pa," Lily called with a smile. She turned and gave me an evil smirk. "See you soon, Reaper." Lily chuckled as she grabbed Junior's hand, and they disappeared into the darkness. Thorn leaned against me and snorted.

"Right at ya, buddy, and good riddance to them," I let out under my breath. I turned to Thorn and knelt down to his level. "Okay, Thorn. What did you want to show me?"

Thorn pawed at a wider crack between some wooden slabs, and I realized something was on the other side.

"Okay, let me see what I can get." I gently moved him over and pulled my sleeves down over my hands to reach through, blindly trusting him, and felt a thick cord. Pulling, it easily came with me back through the opening. *Huh?* "What am I supposed to do with this? Pull it?" I asked and yanked it, but nothing happened. Thankfully, it wasn't a makeshift alarm on the cage. I guess I should have thought of that sooner. Thorn snapped his teeth at me before pointedly looking at the cord, and I chuckled at his meaning.

"Yeah, I'll just go-go gadget my razor-sharp teeth to saw through this." I snorted and rolled my eyes. "We have no idea what's on this, so I'm not using my teeth," I said, eyeing Thorn. "But... we can use YOU."

Thorn backed up with wide eyes and slammed into the back of the cage. "Don't worry, Thorny... since this is all your fault for not smelling the intruders, you're not getting any more snacks if we live through this," I said.

I got the desired effects as he exploded with his namesake. His skin lengthened along with his armor into sharp points along his back and legs. He curled his lips in a snarl, and I cocked my head at him. "See, now you can help if you get your ass over here."

I reached over and grabbed the edge of his armor, pulling him closer to the rope. "Hold still," I instructed and started to saw through the cord with one of his spikes. As it snapped, we noticed it loosened the board but not enough to allow us our freedom. If anything, I thought we had just found a way out. I just hoped it was in time.

A sharp whistle cut through the silence and pulled my attention away from our process.

"Family, gather around for our Priestess Julia Brown."

As they passed and gathered on one side of the fire, figures walked out from the shadows and dropped objects into the cauldron. I counted ten altogether: men, women, and a few children if I went by their height. They held hands and started to chant, swaying their bodies to the haunting melody.

The slight breeze that was coming from the south suddenly stopped and changed direction, becoming stronger and bringing larger raindrops. The wooden planks of our cage started to groan as the wind whipped through them. The sound of the small bones clinking could be heard over the shack's lone window—until everything stopped all at once. It was as if the world was frozen in time. No noise, movement, breeze, or rain. It was as if a dome had been placed over us, concealing us. I glanced down at Thorn and realized we were the only ones that were unaffected.

I kept my voice down as I leaned back into Thorn. "Well, I don't know what's going on, but I'm not waiting to find out." I reached for another cord to saw through as a faint guitar melody reached my ears. A door slammed, pulling my attention away once again to see the famous Julia Brown herself exiting the shack. Dressed in a simple white gown, she seemed to float along the ground toward the frozen LaComb family. As she got closer to the firelight, I could make out her features.

She had dark hair piled on the top of her head, with a few locks falling along her jawline. Along the front of her dress was a row of bones that ran the width of her chest and draped down to her petite waist. From what I could see, she wore no shoes but moved as one would stroll along a park.

Who is this woman?

The first person she came to was Lily's father. She touched his cheek as a mother would a child and gave him a soft smile before kissing his forehead and breaking the spell of the wind and rain. As she moved to the next living statue, her haunting words were carried on the wind as it became stronger, as if her own words gave it power.

· · ·

"Go to sleep, you little baby
      Rest now, you obeyed me.
Your work's all done, and your final rest's begun
I'll leave your body for the daisies.

You're a sweet little baby
      You've never truly loved, I despised thee.
I tricked you too, and now I start anew
I'll leave your body for the daisies.

You're a sweet little baby
      The time has come, so praise be.
The taste of despair, it's all in the air
I'm gonna swaddle it up like a baby.

Don't you weep, pretty baby
      I was always pretty crazy.
It 'tis the hour that I need more power
Gonna need another lovin' baby.

Go to sleep, you little baby
      Go to sleep, my little baby.
You and me, and the devil make three
Don't need no one but to slay thee."

An arch of light slashed out from her hand and decapitated all the LaCombs around the fire, punctuating the end of the verse. I choked back a silent scream as I watched, their bodies remaining to stand and slightly swaying as she continued singing.

"C ome now and repay me
    My sweet little priceless baby.
Come and lay your bones on the obsidian stones
And be my every lovin' baby."

T he bodies clumsily stumbled over each other towards the tall weeds without their heads, where there indeed was a slab of rock laid out, and they all lay down and stopped moving. She let out a sharp whistle and casually began to pick up the decapitated heads, throwing them into the cauldron.

Movement in the tall grass had me shuffling away from the edge of the cage right as a massive alligator shot out of the dark. Two more joined it as they descended on the freshly departed LaComb family.

"Thorn, I think we might be in more trouble than I had originally calculated."

CHAPTER 11
Three's a Crowd

Ravena

If it weren't for a couple of Kaye's darts, it would have been almost impossible to tell where to go from the bone pit of horrors in the dark. A small part of me was ecstatic that I was on the right path, but I was more worried than anything else. Kaye wasn't the type to leave her weapons lying around, not even as a trail. We were taught to leave other landmarks like broken plant limbs or dragging our feet when being led somewhere. The fact that her darts were carelessly dropped meant someone else had her weapons, and these were dropped by mistake. I picked them up and carefully placed them in my inner pocket as I continued on.

It wasn't long until I heard a faint haunting melody that I changed my direction to follow, keeping my steps light.

I know what you're thinking. Dark swamp, check. Deadly creatures, check. Why the hell am I going TOWARD the creepy noise? Simple. It's. My. JOB!

As I slowly approached, something grabbed my attention, causing me to pause. A scuffling noise came from behind me and to the left. No way in hell was I going to allow something to get the drop on me. I eased back and squatted down to see what was out here with me.

As I got closer, moans could be heard. "Ahh. Yes, baby. Right there."

"Yeah, come on this thick dick."

"I'm coming."

Well, I guess that explains what was making the scuffling noise.

No need to stay here and ruin their night as a Peeping Tom.

"I love you, Junior."

"Love you too, now let's hurry back."

Wait a second, was that *our* Junior? The creep at the old house?

"I don't trust that Reaper alone."

"Oh, don't worry. I'm sure Julia has already taken care of her. But I agree." An arc of light flared across the sky. She gasped. "Shit. We need to hurry."

"Yeah, we shouldn't 've run off," Junior commented.

"But it was worth it," the woman giggled.

I quickly and quietly followed them as they ran past me and toward the melody. I had the pleasure of Junior flashing me his ass the whole way as he tried to get his overalls back on.

Junior and the girl who looked way too young to be with him burst through the hedge of weeds and into a clearing. A simple shack was the only building that stood out in this bayou. *That must be Julia's shack we've been looking for.* The deranged couple slowed to a walk and looked around the area as they approached the cauldron over the open fire pit. I could only assume the woman dressed in white who was attending the fire was none other than Julia Brown. The Bone Witch definitely lived up to the name—dressed in white and covered in bones. She had an ethereal glow about her as she hummed and stirred whatever was in the cauldron.

Well, I found the witch. Now, where's Kaye and Thorn?

I tried reaching out for him again as I scanned the area, but I got a sharp stabbing pain between my eyes as if I slammed into a wall. There had to be something blocking us. I spotted a cage in the back right corner of the clearing just out of the light that I was hoping my friends were stuck in, so I made my way over as I grasped some of the conversation.

"Priestess, where's my family?" the woman asked.

"Lily, my sweetie child. They are serving me in other ways. Just as you will have to."

I didn't know what she meant, nor did I want to know. I was on a mission to first find my friends.

"Thorn, stop wiggling." Kaye's words allowed me to smile finally.

They were alive, and that meant I could focus on a rescue. That cage must have been spelled somehow, and that was why I couldn't reach Thorn. I snuck up close enough to whisper. "But he's more fun when he does."

"Jesus!" Kaye grabbed her chest and glared at me. "Took your time finding us."

"Sheesh. Sorry. Apparently, something is blocking my connection with Thorn; otherwise, I would have been here sooner. Need some help?"

Kaye arched a perfect eyebrow and rolled her eyes before grabbing the cord she had dropped before I scared her. She continued to cut it against Thorn's sharpened skin spikes.

It's cool to finally see those things come in handy instead of causing destruction in my room.

"I think the cage is spelled," she explained as she finished with that cord.

"Here," I said, pulling my last knife and handing it to her.

"You cut this as I pull." I stood up and grabbed hold of the edge of the wooden plank, pulling as hard as I could. She reached out and grabbed the last cord that was keeping the plank firmly in place when suddenly an arm came around my neck, tearing me away from my friends.

Immediately, I tucked my chin down and grabbed the arm with both hands.

"I knew you would show up." Junior's rotten breath wafted over my skin. "Not so feisty now that you're in my neck of the bayou, huh?"

"Funny you would say that," I said as I stepped to the side and brought my left fist back as hard as I could, making solid contact with his crotch.

"Ugh."

He bent over but didn't loosen his grip, so I struck and lifted my elbow up as fast as I could and was rewarded with a crack of his nose.

"Fuck." He grunted and released his hold, and I spun around to face the asshole that apparently was in on this to begin with. "You cunt!" he screamed and kicked out.

I easily dodged his attack and almost felt sorry for him. There had to be a reason why he was on this side of shit instead of actually helping us get control of the situation here. A banshee shrill cut through the night's downpour before something landed on my back and started to pummel away.

"Leave my husband alone!"

Okay, so the psycho bitch explained Junior. He got attached to the hypnotic pussy.

'Hey, Rave, did you know you had a monkey on your back?' Thorn chuckled.

'Oh, thanks. Here I thought I was just getting old,' I grunted out, catching sight of him as he ran past. *"Hey, where are you going?'* I reached back and grabbed something solid and pulled, flipping said monkey over me.

I heard a thump and a scream before I got my answer. "Ahhh. Get this animal off me!" Junior yelled.

I was tempted to look myself, to see what damage he was doing, until I heard a distinctive click.

"Don't move." The small cold barrel pressed against my temple was a good indication that a gun was trained on me. "Stand up slowly."

I did as she said, and she turned me towards the cage, completely ignoring the scuffle behind us. I could feel her smaller frame shaking through my jacket as she pressed against me and used me as a human shield.

"Where's your friend at?" Daisy Sunshine asked as she pressed harder on the gun. It felt like she was hoping to just magically push it inside my head. *Newsflash, woman, it doesn't work that way.*

"Last I saw her, she was in the cage," I said blankly.

"Call her," she demanded.

"On the phone?" I asked, keeping my voice monotone, and I could feel the girl's frustration as she let out a sigh.

"No, you bitch. I have her phone. See?" I felt the girl shift behind me and lifted Kaye's phone over my right shoulder, strong and steady. I slightly moved my head to get a better look at the left hand that was holding the gun and noticed it slightly shaking.

Hmm. So, she's right-handed, after all.

"Any particular thing you want me to tell her?" I asked, looking forward back at the cage.

"Just call 'er name so she'll come out," she snapped.

"Okaaay." I took a deep breath because what I was about to do would either be great or the last thing I would do on this earth. "Lyrical!" I called.

When we were kids, Kaye and I used to talk about what we would do if we ever found ourselves taken hostage when we one day became Reapers. Our badass eleven-year-old selves believed we could outsmart our attackers. Depending on our codeword, we would let our partner know which hand the weapon was in and if we gave our consent to be stupid. *Yep, I was being stupid*.

I heard it flying through the air before pain exploded in my left shoulder. *Fuck!* Thankfully, the move was ingrained over time with as much practice as Kaye and I had done over the years. It was supposed to be simple, a straight shot into that bitch's hand knocking the gun free. Instead, I got impaled by my own knife, but I wasn't the only one if I went by the hysterical crying behind me.

"Shit, I'm sorry, Rave!" Kaye called, running out from the shadows.

I turned to face my attacker when she yanked her wrist from the back of my shoulder, causing more damage and both of us to cry out. As she held her wrist to her chest, I noticed she no longer had her gun, so I gritted my teeth and pulled the knife out of my shoulder. I'm no doctor, but at least my training included basic anatomy, and I didn't think it hit the bone. *Lucky for me.* Blinking away the tears that obscured my vision, I saw Miss Bitch reaching for the gun.

"You bitch. You'll pay for that," she wailed, raising the gun and taking aim at Kaye.

I didn't hesitate. I reached back to throw my knife, but she suddenly disappeared. She screamed from my left, and I caught sight of her as she was dragged away and into the nearby swamp.

"What the fuck just happened?"

"Must have been one of the alligators," Kaye said as she picked up her gun and checked the ammo. "There are at least two more gators that I saw, but one of them is massive. Shit. I only have three more bullets."

Thorn let out a grunt as he slammed into the base of a tree.

'Thorn!'

Shit, he's probably knocked out cold.

Junior smiled down at him as he moved aggressively toward him.

Bang!

"Okay... two bullets left," Kaye said as Junior collapsed to the ground with a hole through his neck and blood pouring out.

"Remind me not to get on your bad side." I chuckled and put pressure against my shoulder. *Fuck that was going to smart later.*

"You could never." She grinned.

'Rave, I hurt my leg,' Thorn whined as he tried to stand and began limping our way.

"What's wrong with Thorn?"

"His leg is fucked up." I shrugged in frustration and bit my bottom lip as pain shot down my arm with the gesture. Suddenly catching sight of movement low to the ground, I pointed to the area behind him with my good arm, "Shit!"

Kaye raised her gun and took aim, hitting the alligator behind Thorn. Smartly, it turned, fleeing back into the grass.

We ran over to check on Thorn.

"Looks like a bad sprain," I said.

"I can try and splint it," Kaye wondered as she looked around. I didn't know what the hell she was going to use. I didn't see her bag anywhere or extra clothes. "Oh! I can use the shirt Junior had hanging through his belt loop," she announced, running off toward the corpse. *At least he was being useful.*

"Here, Thorn, lie down so you don't injure yourself more," I coaxed my stubborn friend. Within a few moments, Kaye was back with cloth from Junior's unused shirt and a few twigs. "Here. For your shoulder." I didn't have time to really deal with my own shoulder, so I just pressed the wadded-up cloth between my bra strap and shoulder and hoped it stayed. We wrapped his leg to the best of our ability and helped him back up.

'Think you can walk at least?' I asked, worried he wouldn't be able to and we might have to carry him.

'Yeah, but Rave... we have a bigger problem.' Fear seeped into Thorn's tone.

'What do you mean?'

But before he could answer, I could hear it. Chanting.

I looked over my shoulder and found Julia swaying back and forth, head tilted back and her arms held above her. Darker clouds were gathering and swirling in the sky.

"We're in trouble," Kaye observed.

'Rave, they took Kaye's bag. I think it might be inside that shack,' Thorn worried.

"Shit!" We needed that bag. Kaye always carried extra ammo, plus she had medical supplies in there. Given what we had dealt with already, we needed it desperately.

Kaye looked between Thorn and Julia. She hesitated for a brief moment and looked torn between helping Thorn or needing to go after Julia.

"Here! Try and delay her!" I encouraged, handing her the two tranqs I found on the way here. "Thorn thinks your bag is in the shack. We're going to go get it."

Kaye nodded and took off in the witch's direction as I carefully picked up Thorn. Pain shot through my left shoulder, but I held back my complaints and picked up my best friend. He was still thorned out, and even with my jacket covering me, those could be deadly if he added any sudden pressure against them. I wasn't looking forward to playing a kabob.

'Keep an eye on Kaye for me, okay?' I let out a wheeze as he rolled into me, his spikes digging against my coat. *'Can you*

turn off the spikes? They're starting to hurt.' Okay, so most of my complaints.

'You know I can't when I'm agitated like this.'

He had a point. I sucked it up and moved as fast as I could, focusing on the shack even though I heard Kaye's gun going off.

'Her tranqs aren't doing anything, Rave. It's like hitting a forcefield around the bitch,' Thorn informed me.

I shot a quick glance Kaye's way and saw the two tranqs floating in the air less than six inches away from Julia's torso. We reached the shack's entrance, and I sat Thorn down.

"Little Reaper. Did ya really think I would make it that easy to get to me?" Julia's accent was thick and sultry as she turned and smiled at Kaye.

'Rave! Gator!' Thorn yelled, and like an English Pointer, pointed out the alligator slinking toward Kaye.

'Go find her bag. I got her,' I told Thorn, taking off towards my bestie. "Kaye!" I yelled, pulling her attention away from the deranged witch. "Gator." I pointed over her shoulder to the overgrown water lizard, but she couldn't see it from where she was.

Fuck!

I ran my hand over my Demfire bracelet, and Honor came alive, snaking down my arm and extending into a whip. I lashed out in time to snag the gator around the neck before he lunged for Kaye.

"Help Thorn!" I shouted, pulling to the left and trying to hold the gator back. Kaye didn't hesitate but ran straight into the shack, hopefully to find her bag to help take this witch down. A deep bellow sounded from the gator as he continued pulling against me and toward my friends.

What the hell was up with this thing? Wild gators naturally feared people, so either this bad boy was a pet, a shifter, or it was spelled. Either way, he wasn't making this easy on me. He pulled, causing pain to shoot up my left arm, and I almost dropped my whip, causing me to trip over something. I kicked at it and found a femur. *Oh god!*

'*Hurry up, Thorn,*' I mentally urged as I picked up the bone and moved closer to the beast, hitting it over the head. His jaw opened with a hiss, and he turned my way. *Well, that's one way to get his attention.* I went to hit him again and realized a huge chunk of meat was at the bone's end. My stomach rolled, and I was debating dropping the femur right as he lunged for me. His jaws snapped the bone in half, and I fell back with a yelp.

That was a femur, the strongest bone in the body, and he just snapped it like a twig.

'*Rave! Watch out!*' Thorn yelled. I quickly flicked my wrist, unraveling the whip's thong around his neck, and grabbed hold of the handle. With a simple thought, my Demfire whip transformed into a staff right as the gator's jaw came down, jarring my arms in the process.

'*A little help here!*' I shouted.

'*What do you expect us to do? He's obviously not scared of humans,*' Thorn growled back.

My staff had no problem holding against the jaws of life and death, but the pain in my shoulder and my adrenaline weren't going to last forever.

'*Did you find her bag?*' I asked, shifting my weight as the gator tried to get at me once again.

'*Yeah.*'

'*Then have her shoot the fucking lizard! Lead her over here.*'

Thorn started to howl, and I was sure he'd guide Kaye closer, so I had to trust she knew where to shoot this damn thing. She was the smarty pants in this relationship. I knew they went over this shit in class, but I wasn't the type to really pay attention; that's why I had Kaye.

"Shoot it!" I yelled.

A gunshot rang out, and I screamed as the gator charged me. My grip faltered and slipped just when his eyes rolled up, and he collapsed. Dead.

"Holy Shit!" I whispered.

"Rave! Are you okay?" Kaye asked, running over to me and helping me up. Fighting off the gator had exhausted me, and all I wanted to do was sleep, but our mission wasn't done.

"Yeah," I said with some effort. "It was a piece of cake." I smiled and retracted my bracelet.

I caught Julia Brown in my peripheral, and my heart plummeted. She had stopped chanting and trying to bring forth a hurricane and instead had conjured a spell. And it was coming right at Kaye's back. Without thinking, I shoved Kaye out of the way, and the force of the spell sent me sliding across the yard.

'Rave!' Thorn cried.

Besides having the breath knocked out of me, I was fine, physically—just sore. If anything, the bitch was just pissing me off.

"Are you okay?" Kaye asked, giving me a once-over.

I nodded and focused back on Julia as I unwound my bracelet once again.

"Julia Brown. You are hereby charged with evading Purgatory's call, and we are here to return you," Kaye said as we approached.

Julia started to laugh and turned to face us fully, her arms glowing slightly with a sickly green tint. Probably loading up on more spells. If she was going to hit us with spells, that meant her barrier was finally down.

"Sorry, little Reapers, but that won't be happening. Guess you should have had a plan B." She cackled and pulled back her arm.

A crack splintered the night as I flicked my wrist, and Julia's head rolled from her shoulders.

"How's that for plan B?" I asked as I sat down and watched her body topple over while her magic disappeared from her body.

CHAPTER 12

Oopsies, Our Bad

RAVENA

"What happened to us always completing the job, Rave?" Kaye growled at me.

"It's not like she could have stood trial like that," I pointed out.

"True, but don't you think this is overkill?" Kaye asked me as she rolled her eyes at my antics.

I paused as I looked down at the last of the bitch's clothes and the small bones she had around her neck before throwing those into the bonfire as well.

"Nope," I said as I wiped my palms along my jeans. "Think of it as a cleansing of the area." I smiled in her direction before picking up the lighter fluid and proceeding to Julia Brown's shack.

The darkness had receded without the witch and her magic, and the storm clouds were no longer looming. I'm sure if I was listening to the weather report, they would be marking it up to some supernatural voodoo or miracle shit. If they only knew how on the nose they would be.

Standing in front of the small window of the shack, I opened the lighter fluid container and smiled as I doused it with liquid.

"We could have at least finished the job and delivered her corpse there. Who knows what they could have done in Purgatory. They might have been able to put her back together and bring her back. You know, maybe get some answers," she spouted out, and it was my turn to roll my eyes.

"Yeah, right. Like they have Necromancers there. They are extinct for a reason, Kaye," I shot back.

"Okay, forget about the Necro, you're right," Kay conceded. "And I understand the need to cleanse the area and burn her shack, but is burning her body to ashes really necessary?" She followed me around the area, keeping an eye out for any more of Julia's pets.

My jaw dropped as I turned, clutching my chest, and took in my best friend. "Of course it is. The witch tried to have us eaten by her walking alligator closet." Kaye's deadpan look wasn't impressed. "Oh, that reminds me. We need to skin that damn thing. I'm taking it as a souvenir." Kaye sighed, and I sucked on my teeth before looking at her and gave her a sorrowful look. "Look, I know I fucked up. I'm sorry. I really am," I said as she gave me a doubtful look. "But you and I both know it happens on the job. If she would have just come and not fought back, none of this would have happened in the first place. We'll just say it was a code DF5 and call it a day." I shrugged.

'You are hopeless, you know that?' Thorn snorted but didn't leave his spot in the middle of the clearing.

While I chopped up Julia Brown's body and threw her into the fire, Kaye gave Thorn medical attention. Since he had gone through an ordeal, he was too tired to help clean up the place.

'Whose the one that's helpless? At least I can still move with a knife wound in my freaking arm. You have a sprain, so obviously, you're dying,' I pointed out, picking up one of the twigs that we had used for his splint earlier.

Lighting it from the bonfire, I threw it towards the shack and watched in awe as it went up in flames. I took a few minutes to ensure the flames didn't get out of hand before returning to Kaye and her packs of tricks.

"You know Defiant Fucker level 5 isn't a real code right," Kaye said giving me a mocking smirk.

"Yeah. Yeah. But you're the one who knows all the real codes and our made-up ones. That's why you're the smart one in this group," I said, buttering her up to handle this mess. Even though it was my lead, Kaye, I learned the hard way, was the one who could sweet talk the Pope out of his clothes. "Got anything in there that will blow air?"

"Besides my best friend and Thorn?" she sassed back, and my eye roll couldn't be contained.

"Oh, come on, Kaye. I obviously fucked up this assignment, but if I bring back some skin for our dads, it might win us some points," I emphasize.

"You can't fool me. Our parents dote on us like we can do no wrong. This is for you and your petty ass." She gave me a knowing look that I couldn't dispute. *She knows me too well.*

"Okay, fine," I said, pulling my knife free and making a few slits into his arms, behind his head, and waiting for Kaye.

"Here, it's like a little air compressor," she stated, handing me a small hand device.

"Seriously, what all do you have in that fucking bag? It's like a bottomless bag," I say aimlessly.

"It kinda is from what I've been told, but I don't treat it as one. I would never find what I needed if that was the case."

She pulled out some twine and grimaced. "Sorry. I don't have another bag, but you can bundle it up with this."

It was better than nothing. I took it as I looked at the setting sun. *Shit.* We didn't have long before we were plummeted back into darkness.

I wasn't big on hunting, but that didn't mean I hadn't gone with my father before, so I knew how to skin regular animals like deer and wild boar. But this alligator was a new one for me. I assumed it was basically the same thing, though. I figured since the old hag wanted to feed us to her walking alligator collection, Kaye and I could mark this moment with our own belts. Our last mission before becoming full-fledged Reapers.

Using the air compressor, I blew air into its body, elevating the scales as a way to make it easier to skin it. Thankfully, I had him skinned and the scales bundled up in record time.

"What do you plan on doing with all of that anyway?" Kaye asked as she threw her pack over her shoulder.

I made a makeshift sling with the scales, I threw it over my good shoulder and looked at Thorn.

'Sorry, buddy. You're gonna have to limp out of here like the rest of us,' I clarified, only to get a row of gums and teeth as my answer.

He could be upset all he wanted; all of us were injured, and I couldn't carry him.

"I figured we needed something to remember our last mission before our safety net is yanked from us." I smiled as I reached down and grabbed a piece of meat from the skinless alligator. The bonfire I had burned Julia in had died down to embers, so it was nothing to rub a piece of meat in the ashes and throw the meat close to the water.

It landed with a thunk, and moments later, I could see ripples in the water heading our way.

"I think it's time to leave," Kaye said, backing up.

"Yep, I couldn't agree more." At least this way, they could come and eat their own, cleaning up what I'd done.

We turned, and I led the way back to our lanterns, which surprisingly were still in one piece and still lit. We made it back to our floating piece of log, but this time, both Kaye and I used the paddles to maneuver us back down the bayou. It worked out great since I could use my right arm, and her left one wasn't injured, it just took us longer getting back to Jules dock than finding Julia Brown.

"Look! There's his dock!" Kaye cried out, taking a break to wipe the sweat from her brow.

'Thank you, baby Jesus!' Thorn exclaimed and rocked the boat.

"Will you calm down," I chastised him as I pushed our log closer to the dock. Cicada shells lined the edge as I reached out to pull us closer. *Eww.*

'You might be fine stewing in your own filth, but this is disgusting even for me,' Thorn whined.

He had a point. I'd had days where I'd gotten sweaty, dirty, downright disgusting, but this took the prize.

"Do you think Jules will be easy to find?" Kaye asked as she awkwardly climbed onto the deck.

"Hopefully. I don't want to stay around here that long."

As if speaking his name conjured him, the whirling of his wheelchair was heard as he exited the motel. Tiny lights shone along his wheelchair, lighting his way as he came out to greet us. *That's pretty nifty.*

"Here are your lamps," Kaye said in greeting as I tied up his precious heirloom.

I turned to find Jules staring at me with his milky eyes. A chill ran down my spine. He pushed his wheelchair closer to me, and I swallowed hard, forcing myself not to move as he peered up at me.

'Rave... Junior's shirt,' Thorn warned me.

Shit! I still had the bastard's shirt pressed against my wound, which I really needed to get looked at.

It was one thing to fix up Thorn's sprained leg, but I wasn't about to triage my stab wound out in the damn boonies when we could do it back in civilization.

"Um. I can explain," I started, and then Jules surprised me by asking his own question.

"Julia gone?"

"Yes, sir, and your son is gator bait."

"Rave!" Kaye chastised me.

"What?" I shrugged and looked at her. "He needs to know," I said, indicating Jules.

He sucked on his teeth for a moment and gave me a small nod. "No good 'oung'n," he said before pulling out some money. "It all there."

"Sir, you keep it. I know it won't bring back your son, but hopefully, you can use it for other things," Kaye insisted, taking his hand and folding it back over the money.

He nodded slightly before turning and disappearing back into the darkness, his small lights leading him to his home.

'I don't know about you, but I'm not going back through the haunted mansion,' Thorn stated before leading the way around the building.

If I had my way, I would never come back to the damn state. One trip was enough for me.

CHAPTER 13

Voodoo Magic

Ravena

'I *can't believe we're doing this,'* I murmured to Thorn as I yanked my boot out of the mud and leaned against an old cypress tree to put it back on. I whipped my long brunette hair over my shoulder in the hope of relieving the heat off my neck, but it turned out it was pointless in a swamp. *I knew wearing all black was a bad idea.*

'*What, getting a free mud bath?'* He chuckled at my predicament and climbed up the tree I was leaning on.

'*I see your leg is feeling better,'* I noticed.

'*Yep, it's amazing what pain meds and pampering will do for you. I'm telling you. Kaye is a godsend,'* Thorn raved.

'*If I ever find a Genie, I'm asking for Kaye to be able to hear your ass. And then we can see how she treats you.'* I chuckled as I took in his position in the tree. At least he could get to higher ground so I wouldn't be tempted to smack him with my boot.

'*You do that, and I'll piss in your bed,'* he threatened.

'*Go ahead. It's your bed too.'*

No matter what, Thorn was still the grumpy, sarcastic, most unfiltered, and loving bestie I could ask for. I owed him my life. I would have been gator bait a couple of days ago if it weren't for him. Thankfully, after having my injury looked at, I was only coming out of this mission with a scarred and sore shoulder.

I picked up my alligator scales, pushed the Spanish moss out of my way, and finally spotted the decrepit shack before us. The mismatched and uneven wooden planks along the path leading to the wide porch didn't give me much confidence in holding my weight, but I had little choice if I wanted help and some answers from the VooDoo Priestess. I tentatively took a step out, finding the boards stable, and gave Thorn a slight smile before taking another one.

'If we die in this swamp, I'm blaming you and haunting your ass even in the afterlife,' Thorn hissed. His short brown coat bristled as he jumped down onto the edge and cautiously followed behind me.

'Good luck with that,' I chuckled. There was no way he was going to die out here, not with his cowardly capability of getting out of here before something got to him.

The shack was just as the locals said, in the middle of the bayou with a large covered porch and two large windows with white paint peeling off the trim. The tin roof looked to be the only stable item attached to the building besides the beaten-down porch swing. No, even that didn't look durable enough to hold an infant's weight. A gentle breeze brought the sound of the creaky porch swing, along with the smell of moldy wood rot.

This place was a far cry from the city streets in the midwest or even Bourbon Street. The evening sun was setting, but it did nothing to diminish the sweltering heat of the bayou. I was almost second-guessing wearing my black leather jacket, but I loved this thing and didn't trust leaving it behind in the car.

We had finished our job with the Bone Witch a couple of days ago, and our flight back home was arranged for tomorrow morning; this might be my last chance to get some answers from the Seer about what happened. Plus, after talking to some contacts, I was told she or her partner were just the people I was looking for about the alligator belts I wanted as souvenirs.

Earlier, as I stood on the balcony of our Garden District home, I had asked Kaye if she wanted to come with me. As my answer, she started the tub, began to strip, and told me not to take another dip in the bayou.

Friends. Sometimes, you want to shank them.

Honestly, I couldn't blame her. She deserved the royal treatment since I left her explaining what happened to Julia Brown to headquarters. Let's just say I could hear Cassie clearly, and Kaye *wasn't* on speakerphone. We drew out the assignment as long as possible, using our injuries to milk more time before we needed to head back, but graduation was in a few days and we couldn't put off any more time.

As I took in the shack once again, I couldn't help but remember the main reason why I was here. Taking on risk was part of the job, but I'd never experienced a close call, let alone get hit with something I couldn't identify.

'*Eek,*' Thorn screamed and jumped a mile high when something slipped into the water next to us. As a badass carnivore from Madagascar, he sure was a scaredy-cat.

I glanced over and spotted a Nutria swimming across the surface, and let out a nervous laugh as I continued on. A swamp beaver I could handle. At least it wasn't a gator or a snake. I could manage many things, but reptiles were now a no-go for me. I'd had enough on this trip.

A squeal echoed around the swamp, and I jerked my head

back over to where the Nutria was, only to see a gator's tail disappear into the water.

At least it isn't me it was feasting on.

I swallowed the lump in my throat, increasing my pace until we reached the porch and stepped over the red brick dust into Priestess Tanda's shop. Inside, two lazy circling ceiling fans filled the room with synonymous squeaking but did nothing for the inferno of the swamp heat. Closing the door behind us, inside was a glass counter to the right with an old-time cash register on top. Rows of cases furnished the shop, filled with satchels, crystals, vials, and other knickknacks. Who knew what they were for or what to do with 'em. I sure didn't.

"Come on in, young pup," a woman's voice drifted from the back.

"Hello?" I called as Thorn branched off to sniff at a few of the items on the shelves.

"Have a look around, and I'll be right with you, dear," the voice yelled, even though there was no need. Thorn and I were the only ones in the shop.

There was no traffic in this area, especially this late in the evening. In fact, I was warned *not* to venture out this way because of the *monsters* that were seen around here. Funny, since I just took out a big bad just down the road. So, I didn't need their warnings. Monsters were my bread and butter.

If they only knew I was here to see a *monster* of their own making, they would probably run screaming. Priestess Tanda, the seer of life and death, was a powerful monster in her own right. From what I'd been told, she was one of the original Purgatory allies that helped form the N.I.T.R.A's US branch, but she wasn't hands-on anymore. She was more of an informant and no threat to us. Since she worked with our organization, she didn't touch the Bone Witch; she only called in the tip. Instead, I was sent, and now I thought the damn witch's spell did something to me before I ended her since I'd felt off ever since. But I needed the voodoo queen to confirm and hopefully help me out.

On the counter next to me was a box labeled "Moon Soul" with some vials of yellowish-gold liquid and a picture frame. The frame had the words Nerezza scrolled into the silver metal, with a picture of a girl around my age with a white Lynx. I picked up the frame and took a closer look, observing our similarities. We both had sepia skin color and brunette hair. Where my long hair was typically straight, and I had to work to get curls to stay in it, hers looks naturally wild. Her smile was infectious, and just by looking at her, she looked like she would be a lot of fun to be around. I'd often been told I had resting bitch face. Her gray eyes sparkled with mirth, and I found myself a little jealous that I was stuck with my brown eyes. Beauty marks ran along her cheekbones, whereas my face was completely bare of any markings. Still, we could easily pass as cousins, even sisters.

"Ah. So you must be the one that took care of the Bone Witch," a middle-aged red-headed woman said as she walked through a beaded doorway from the back, startling me. I replaced the picture and gave her my full attention. Her hair was pulled back and up into a messy bun, and her bright blue eyes were laser-focused on me, but I had a feeling she didn't miss Thorn as he moseyed around the store. She wore a loose light-green short sleeved V-neck blouse and a flowy white skirt that went down to the tops of her bare feet. The scent of rosemary reached me as she came to stand before me. For a first impression, she left me intrigued. I wasn't expecting the great priestess to look this young and put me at ease so efficiently.

"I didn't have a choice," I murmured under my breath.

"Nonsense..." she quirked her eyebrow in question and gave me a pointed look.

"Ravena," I supplied. She gave me a small, knowing smile

as if she already knew my name. Pfft. For all I know, she probably did.

"Ravena, you always have a choice, dear. Sometimes, we just don't like the consequences of those choices that are presented to us."

"How d—"

"Come now, child, stupid does not look good on you," she chastised me. "I recommend not using that strategy in the future. It will only turn out bad for you." She cocked her head to the side and squinted. "And it seems you're already up Shit Creek without a paddle."

"What do you mean? Did that Bone Witch do something to me?" I asked, hanging on to her words.

"So, what items were you wanting me to make out of the gator skin?" She expertly dodged my question.

"Just two belts. But do you know what she did to me?" I pushed, desperately needing the answer.

She held out her hand and gave me a pointed look. I handed her the sling which held the skins and raised an eyebrow in question.

"There's no such thing as a free meal in the bayou, missy," she said as she walked into another room with my skins, leaving the door open.

Thorn came up to me and gave me a curious look. *'Think it's an invitation?'*

'Has to be because I'm not just letting her keep my damn trophy.' Not letting this opportunity pass me by, I followed her, and Thorn trailed behind me.

"Hey, wait a minute. We have— Woah," I said as we walked into a smaller room.

I really wasn't expecting to see a room from a movie set of a fortune teller. Fairy lights were interspersed around the room, yet I didn't see any strings. The absence of light made the shadowy parts of the room darker and more cozy.

I'll never understand this magic stuff.

Hanging vines and plants lined the upper walls and covered the ceiling mostly, and the pleasant scent of incense wasn't too overpowering. For some reason, it was cooler in here, and I found myself relaxing my shoulders and wiping the last of the sweat from my brow. In the back of the room was a built-in work desk where a pot of something was boiling and ingredients were laid out. A small table was in the middle, with a single glowing lamp and two chairs to sit on.

"I have to keep up the appearance of what's expected," Priestess Tanda confirmed as she laid out the gator skin along a shelf she pulled out of the wall. *Where did that come from?*

"So you really can tell fortunes and help out your patrons?" I asked, sitting down and looking closer at the lamp.

Fuck me. That's a glowing skull, not a lamp!

She grabbed a small jar that glowed and sprinkled it over the skin as she answered. "Of course, why else would people come to me? They could go to any VooDoo practitioner in the quarter, but if they want the *real deal*, they come to me." She worked the skin with her fingers as she mumbled under her breath, and my jaw dropped as I watched part of the hide separate into identical strips, folding upon themselves. She pulled out thick silver and gold thread, waved her hand over them, and turned to face me. Behind her, the thread slowly started to weave itself through the leather.

Yeah. Magic is a whole other thing on its own.

Her eyes shined with mirth as she took me in once again, "But like I mentioned before, there's no such thing as a free meal in the bayou."

"What does that even mean?" I asked as I did a double take and scooted away from the ivory skull that once held muscle and flesh and moved in lively ways.

'*It means nothing is entirely free, Rave,*' Thorn uttered as he sniffed at one of the plants by his feet.

"You have a smart one there," she commented.

My eyebrows disappeared into my hairline as I took in her words. "How—"

"My granddaughter, Nerezza, has a special connection to her...let's just call him her *familiar*," she admitted as she leaned against the shelf behind her. *Does that mean Nerezza is a Reaper?* "Don't worry. I can't hear your conversation. I can just see the connection between you two, and your face is very expressive. Plus, I can see the blessing that allows you to speak to him."

Wow. I wasn't expecting all of that.

"The girl in the photo? Is she around?" I asked hopefully. *Maybe I'll get some straight information out of her.* I had a feeling this crazy old bat was gonna run me around in a circle if I was not careful.

She held her chin in her hands and smiled up at me from under her lashes. "Would you like to talk about your issues, or did you come all this way to talk about Nerezza?"

"Ugh. Fine. Me," I grunted out. *Why is this fucking frustrating?*

'Because she's a black widow, and you're falling into her web!' Thorn mocked.

'Not. Helpful,' I spat out.

"Now I'm assuming this visit to my abode isn't agency sanctioned, so let's talk about payment," she said, going for the jugular.

I knew this visit would probably empty my savings. "How much money do you want? I can transfer it as soon as I get service," I admitted as I pulled out my phone to write down the amount in the note section.

She cackled like a true witch and waved away my attempt to get her information.

"I don't need money. If I wanted, I could fund three presidential elections a year for the rest of my long life and then some," she said, standing again and grabbing a small box and a thick piece of parchment paper that smelled like old books.

By the looks of the shack on the outside, I highly doubted that, but who was I to call her a liar.

"What I want is a blood promise to help me at a time of my choosing. In exchange, I will tell you what I know of the Bone Witch, what she's done to you, and how you can fix it," she said, looking over at me and placing the blank parchment paper on the table between us.

I looked down as she waved her hand, and what she just said appeared in black ink across the page. "How will I know it's a one-time deal?" I asked, needing something in writing to ensure I was protected as well.

"As you wish," she said with a faint smile, adding that.

This is a one-time service for both parties.

"Are the belts included in this deal, or are you going to ask for my firstborn next?" I gave her a pointed look.

She matched it and waved her hand once more, adding in the cost of the two belts.

"I want them spelled for protection," I demanded.

Priestess Tanda leaned on the table and placed her chin in her palm.

"Now, little miss picky. You keep demanding, and I'll take out the clause of this being a one-time thing," she countered.

I gave her a small smirk and leaned back in my chair.

"You're the one that's asking for a *blood promise* and for a get-out-of-jail-free card that doesn't expire... well, until I die, but I'm sure you have a way of collecting that even at that point."

The twinkle in the woman's eye confirmed my suspicion.

"As you wish," she said, and added my protection spell. "Now, if you agree, prick your finger with the dagger and spill blood onto the document, and I'll do the same." She opened the box, and a small black dagger rested inside on red velvet.

'What do you think, Thorn? Am I missing anything?' I picked up the document and brought it down so he could observe it.

'Well, the only thing you're missing is your goddamn mind!' he yelled through our link. *'Rave, you should have talked to your parents before coming here. You know, since they are in charge and have more knowledge about this kind of stuff. Or maybe just passed on the Bone Witch to begin with. I told you we should have taken backup for this job. What do you think Kaye would be telling you right now?'* He rolled his eyes and stood up, propping his paws on the table to peek over the edge.

I clenched my jaw because nothing he suggested was helping me *now*. That was all said and done. *'You know how much I hate working with others. Besides, we work best when it's just us and Kaye,'* I admitted, replacing the parchment and picking up the knife.

I quickly poked the pad of my index finger, squeezing out a drop of blood. Once it hit the paper, the blood vanished with a hiss, and out of the smoky peppermint tendril of black smoke, my name was revealed in red. Priestess Tanda did the same, and her name appeared shortly after mine. Without ceremony, the document vanished with a puff of black smoke.

"You can lead a horse to water, but you can't make her drink. Remember that, young master," she said, looking at Thorn.

"I thought you couldn't hear our conversation," I probed.

She chuckled. "I can't, but I don't have to be a mind reader to see the glare he's sending you. Perhaps he's not happy that you took on the witch by yourself or with only your one friend? Too proud to ask for more help? He's right. There's no shame in asking for help," she pointed out. And she was right. They both were.

Thorn was glaring at me for those exact reasons.

"Yeah, yeah, yeah. I'm asking for the help *now*. Can we get onto what that psychotic witch did to me?" I whined.

"Oh, that's simple. Just by looking at your gray aura at your edges, I can tell she's placed a nasty curse on you. But give me your hand so I can see what the specifics of it are per se and what we can do to set you right as rain."

Just my fucking luck. I knew she did something to me.

I gave her my hand and waited for the verdict. Her soft, warm hands turned mine over a few times as she studied my palm. For a brief moment, my hand went cold, and a chill went up my arm before she released it. Discouragingly, she sucked on her teeth and smacked her lips as if she tasted something bad.

"Well, dear, she popped you with a doozy. We call it the Phases of Death. But have no fear." She gave me a reassuring smile as she grabbed a small leatherbound book off of a stool by her. "There are a few ways to disperse it," she said as she flipped to a page I couldn't read at all.

Is that another language?

"Probably the easiest would be to ask her *nicely* to remove it, but the fact she hit you with it, to begin with, doesn't speak highly of that probability. So, counting that out—the next would be to take one of her bones, a small one preferably, like a finger, and boil it into a potion. I can have that ready for you in a week's time. Then you just drink it, and violà. Fit as a fiddle!"

Lead plummeted in my stomach as she explained the process for multiple reasons. One: she wanted me to drink the witch's finger water? Uh...gross. Two:...

"Umm. What if the bones aren't an option?" I asked, feeling myself go clammy.

"Oh. Squeamish? I didn't picture you as one of those, but I guess every agency has to have one," she pondered. "The only alternative since you're against the bone potion is either to have someone bring her back from Purgatory and force her to reverse the curse or you find someone strong enough to cure you," she said as she laced her fingers together.

"Fuck me." The words slipped out of my lips.

Priestess Tanda clacked her tongue and gave me a knowing look. "Let me guess. You killed her instead of detaining and sending her through a door."

I let out a long sigh and bowed my head. The fact was, I hadn't just killed the witch; I burned her to a crisp and fed her to her damn pet alligators. She was okay feeding us to that walking belt, shoes, and briefcase before Kaye turned the tables around. It was only fair. *How in the hell did I fuck up so bad?*

I glanced up and saw the disappointment in her eyes, and she opened her mouth to say something else, but I held up my hand and stopped her. She was either going to blow my mind further or express how much I fucked up, and I already knew that. "What does this Phases of Death curse do exactly?" Maybe it wasn't as bad as it sounded.

"Well...it attacks the victim in phases. The first phase is bad luck. That can be anything from your hair tie breaking to your car dying after just being serviced. The next phase is Pain. Think of headaches or body aches and go from there. The third phase is a beacon. Anything that you're hiding from will be able to find you. Debt collectors, exes, or, in your case... monsters. And the final stage is death," she said with pity in her eyes.

"How long does all of that typically take?"

"Normally, years. The last person I knew with that curse took four years before they even knew something was wrong. They came to me for a good luck charm, and that's how I found they were cursed instead. They were still in the bad luck phase."

"So, there's no hope? I'm a walking, talking corpse?" I asked, dread quickly replacing the hope I once had.

"Well, there is one other way. Not sure if you're willing, but it at least might help with the side effects until you find another Bone Witch to undo the spell or someone strong enough to cure it."

I perked up and gave her a cautious stare. "What's the alternative?" *I highly doubt I'll find another Bone Witch, but maybe I'll find someone along my line of work that's strong enough to cure me.*

"Even though you're a Reaper, a step above human, you've obviously been Angel blessed to have the connection with your pet, like a familiar. Therefore, you might be able to disperse your curse onto multiple partners to the point that it equals out, and no one will feel the ill effects shortening your life."

My jaw dropped at what she was hinting at. "What do you mean partners? I already have my best friends, Kaye and Thorn, as my partners." I pointed to Thorn, who was now giving me a horrified look.

'Yeah, yeah, I know. You can yell at me later,' I cut Thorn off before he could yell at me. One crisis at a time.

She peered at Thorn and smiled before getting up and going back to the belts.

Really? She's going to walk away at a time like this. Maybe her granddaughter, Nerezza, I think her name was... ran away. She was tired of her grandmother running her around in circles too.

She pulled out some metal pieces and fiddled around the belt as she began talking.

"Your best friend and Thorn are considered your family. They are not the type of relationships that are needed to disperse the curse. If that was the case, curses wouldn't be a thing since most people choose their family ties over their blood relations."

She reached for another book from her shelf, turned to a page, bowed her head over the belts, and began chanting and running her hand over the leather. A slight wind breezed through the room, and the skull's flame flickered as she swayed to her own words. The hairs on my skin rose, and Thorn shuffled closer to me and whined.

'Is it supposed to get colder in here?'

'No clue, but don't you have fur on?' I shot back.

'Doesn't mean I don't feel *anything. Sheesh.'*

Just as fast as the wind came, it receded, and Priestess Tanda turned and handed me the two belts with a smile.

"As it's stated in the contract." She sat down in front of me and raised an eyebrow as I took in our belts. As I inspected them, I noticed they had a slight fluorescent change in color.

"Are my eyes going bad, or are these belts changing color?" I confirmed as I turned them and watched as they shimmered from black to a slight green.

"You didn't specify which protection you wanted, so I threw a Hail Mary." She cackled and winked at me before leaning onto the table. "Now, back to your dilemma. I mean sexual. In the Supernatural world, we have mates," she said with a smile in her tone.

I'd done my time in school and learned all about how the supernatural creatures mated and how they had multiple consenting partners.

I didn't even have a steady boyfriend, nor do I want one, and she wants me to have multiple? I barely tolerated Walker as my fuck buddy and—

"Oh, hell no!" I said, hitting the table and propelling myself from the chair. "If that's all you have to say, I think we're done here. If it's a curse that comes in phases, I can handle it. It gives me time to find another Bone Witch or someone with the power to remove it." I looked down at Thorn and motioned for him to come along. "We're out of here."

'I really think we need to tell someone about this,' Thorn butted in, blocking my path.

'Are you serious? They would take us off Reaper status faster than you could sneeze,' I hissed.

"Our deal is still sealed, but I would listen to your tiny genesis," Priestess Tanda called out.

"Yeah, whatever. Thanks for the help... not!" I said childishly as we headed to the front door. My boots stomped a little harder as I marched out of the back room. That was a waste of time. A curse with phases that I could cure by taking on more infuriating men in my life? Yeah right? How many dicks could cure a death curse? Let's see... none... because more than one would fucking drive me bonkers. I would more than likely stab a dick if it was attached to a body that had a running mouth.

Almost to the door, I did a double take of the picture that said Nerezza and wondered how she handled her certifiable grandmother. *I swear, if I ever met her, I'm going to ask how she did it.* As soon as I opened the front door and stepped down and onto the path, I heard her last words.

"Your perfect storm has a cloud with a silver lining. It just requires you to bite the bullet."

I looked back to snap out a question as to what she meant, but her shop was gone. The only thing there was the wooden floorboards on which her shop was once settled.

Fuck me.

Afterword

I hope you enjoyed Ravena's prequel to the N.I.T.R.A's series. This is one series I cannot wait to tackle and see how it intwines with Rez's story. If you haven't had the chance to read Nerezza's story, this is the perfect time to hop on over and pick it up.

I would love to hear your thoughts on this series, good, bad, indifferent, or that it's way too short lol. The best way to do that is by leaving me a review on the platform that you read this on. I enjoy hearing from you and the reviews help me out immensely.

Thank you for reading and taking a chance on me.

Acknowledgments

First of all, I want to thank Jillian for being my PA. You've been keeping me straight when I started to tumble down the rabbit hole. I can't wait to see what we come up with next! I love you to death, bestie!

I also want to thank Kayleigh for staying with me as my Social Media PA. I would be lost without you and your advice. Please don't leave me.

To my *Bossy Minion*, thank you for putting up with my past/present writing chaos. One of these days I'll get it right, until then, you get the pleasure of constantly fixing my mess! LOOOVE you!

Kadee, thank you for the amazing book cover. She's gorgeous.

To my betas: Naedrax (Horror queen) Rb, Becca (Cheerleader) Sabala, Tanya (Eagle Eye) Courtney, Jacquie (Thirsty) Stolz, and Courtney Davis. You girls crack me up, keep me going, and throw out the best ideas. Please don't leave me!

To my ARC team, you guys are the freaking best! You guys blow me away with your energy and how you're always ready to go at a drop of a hat! Thank you!!

Special Shoutouts to:

I also want to thank Rosa Lee, Kira Roman, and Lexie Winston. You guys continue to provide me with a plethora of information and friendship that I don't know what I would do without you.

And finally to my family and friends that have supported me in the process. To my Aunt Patty who has been one of my biggest supporters and is constantly asking me how my book is coming along, thank you. Thank you mom and Nay Nay. I love and miss you both. Fishy kisses. And to the real MVP that pushes me to my computer chair and tells me to write...my Kaeden James. Thank you for being awesome! I love you, little man.

About the Author

Kerry Keller has an addiction to caffeine, swearing, sarcasm, and has no filter when talking in public. As an avid reader to escape the drama the world throws at us, she finally got the bug to write a story she would love to read herself.

When not writing books, you can find her working in women's health care, in college, or being a single mother to a very sarcastic pre-teen boy. She swears she's a bad influence to him, so if you cross paths in the future with him... #sorrynotsorry.

Stalk Me,
It'll be a blast!

Come join the reader group to talk about the world of Purgatory Prep, get sneak peeks, and see what's to come next.

Lynx's Minxes-KK's Reading Group:
http://www.facebook.com/groups/kkslynxsminxes

Join my newsletter for teasers:
https://landing.mailerlite.com/webforms/landing/t5m6a6

TikTok:
https://www.tiktok.com/@kerrykellerauthor

GoodReads:

https://www.goodreads.com/author/show/20923324.
Kerry_Keller

Instagram:
https://www.instagram.com/authorkerrykeller/

Also by Kerry Keller

World of Purgatory

Road to Redemption

Scorned by Hell

Road to Salvation